MILES

A SAVAGE KINGS MC NOVEL

LANE HART

D.B. WEST

COPYRIGHT

Edited by Angela Snyder
Cover by Marianne Nowicki of www.PremadeEbookCoverShop.com

WARNING: THIS BOOK IS NOT SUITABLE FOR ANYONE UNDER 18. PLEASE NOTE THAT IT CONTAINS VIOLENT SCENES THAT MAY BE A TRIGGER FOR INDIVIDUALS WHO HAVE BEEN IN SIMILAR SITUATIONS.

DO YOU LOVE FREEBIES?

If so, click here to sign up for Lane and D.B.'s newsletter to get updates on new releases, discounts and awesome freebies!

SYNOPSIS

Who could ever fall in love with a cold-blooded killer like me?

The answer is no one.

That's why I'm giving up trying to find a woman who wants me for more than one rowdy night. I'm determined to find a wife instead.

If I buy a mail order bride, then she'll have no choice but to stick around. Besides, I have plenty of money to spend thanks to all the successful Savage Kings MC legal and outlaw enterprises.

Kira's the perfect woman, and she's just as eager as I am to tie the knot. I didn't ask why she needed half a million dollars; and honestly, I didn't really care.

Maybe I should have.

A few weeks after Kira becomes my wife, I find myself in the middle of her family's fallout with the Russian mafia.

When I shoot first and ask questions later, I unknowingly drag the entire MC into the crossfire.

Now the Russians are pissed and are out for blood. But they've screwed with the wrong man this time.

The Kings will do whatever it takes to protect their own, no matter the consequences.

And now that Kira is mine, I'll gladly kill anyone who tries to hurt her.

CHAPTER ONE

Miles

"YOU KNOCK SASHA UP YET?" I hear Abe ask Chase from where he's standing over him, spotting for his buddy as Chase powers through a rep of bench presses. I'm on the other side of the room alone, straining the muscles in my tattooed arms and down my back as I struggle to get my chin over the pull-up bar just a few more times.

It's not much, but we have a decent workout room in the basement of the Savage Asylum with all of the standard weight lifting equipment.

"Nah. You knocked up Mercy?" Chase responds as the chrome bar maxed out with weight that he's pressing clangs back down into the holder.

"Hell no," Abe grumbles, sounding oddly disappointed. That doesn't make any sense to me; I've spent my entire life trying *not* to get a woman pregnant.

"Sasha's doc says we might be fucking too much," Chase informs his best friend. I wait for Abe's deep chuckle before he replies with something along the lines of "there's no such thing as fucking too much", because that is the obvious response.

Instead, Abe says, "No shit? Maybe that's our problem too. I'll tell Mercy. God knows my dick could use a break."

"Mine too," Chase agrees. "Every morning I wake up to Sasha riding me before my eyes open. And then at night she wants to go at it as many times as I can get it up. I can't keep performing under all this goddamn pressure!"

That's it.

I can't listen to another fucking word of their ridiculous conversation.

Dropping from the pull-up bar and landing on the soles of my booted feet, I march over to the weight bench and wave my finger back and forth between them. "You two are idiots. Are you seriously bitching like pussies about *too* much sex? There is no such thing!"

"Man, if you only knew," Abe says to me, his dark eyes serious. "Fucking isn't fun when you know your old lady is gonna cry a river a few days later if you didn't make the damn stick thing say she's pregnant!"

"Amen, brother," Chase says, sitting up on the bench to turn around and offer him a fist bump. "I hate disappointing Sasha. Every. Fucking. Month. And now we find out that we fuck too much. But if we fuck too little, she won't get knocked up either. What's the perfect amount of fucking?"

"No idea, man. No idea." Abe mutters as he wipes away sweat from his forehead.

"You're married and you get sex whenever you want. I don't understand the problem. Do you know how lucky you are?" I ask them. "I need to find an old lady. Sasha or Mercy got any friends?"

"None that we would ever tell you about," Chase replies with a grin.

"Screw you," I say while flipping him off. "You both get to fuck your wives all the time without rubbers and still not put a kid in her. That sounds like heaven."

"No, it's hell," Abe argues. "Making a kid is not as easy as you think. And as the man, it's all up to me! I feel like one of those street monkeys and my owner is always saying, 'Dance, Monkey! Dance!' Well, dancing isn't fun when you *constantly* fail at it."

"I have no fucking idea what you're talking about," I tell him.

"You can't understand unless you've been there," Chase says as he strokes his auburn beard.

"Fine. Sign me the hell up! Where can I find an old lady who wants to fuck 24/7?" I ask. It sounds like married life has more perks than I would have expected.

Growing up, my mother nagged the shit out of her first three husbands, none of which were my father, until they eventually gave up and left her. Since I moved out of the house and joined the Marines sixteen years ago, she's been married at least three more times. Maybe her marriages were not the norm after all.

Chuckling, Chase says, "Sorry, bro, but there's not like a catalogue of women or any stores out there that will build the perfect woman and then ship her to you. You've got to go out and search for her."

"Yeah, and it's not easy even after you find her," Abe adds. "There's always shit going down, so you have to find someone to stick around even when things are fucked seven ways to Sunday."

"How do you know if they'll stick around, though?" I ask. That was something my mother couldn't ever seem to figure out.

"You don't," Chase answers. "It's just a chance you have to be willing to take when you feel like you can't live without them."

Fuck, why can't wives and marriages be easier? They should come with a set of rules or something, ones that say you have to be in it for the long haul no matter how bad things get or how fucked up the man is. Something that's more certain than a few vows spoken in a church. Hell, everyone seems to break those fuckers.

Most of my brothers are like Chase and Abe, starting to settle down with one woman. I never understood the benefits until now when it's been weeks since I've gotten laid or even had a blowjob. It'd be nice to have someone wake me up riding my cock before my eyes open every morning. And if she wants sex at night too? Fuck yes. Sign me the hell up for *all* of that.

Too bad I'm not the type of man anyone wants to marry.

I'm a cold-hearted killer with a dirty mouth and a filthy, fucked-up mind. Love and romance haven't ever been even the smallest blips on my radar. They never will be either, because I'm incapable of both.

The only things I have to offer a woman are tons of money, thanks to the Kings' outlaw way of life, and all the hardcore fucking they could ever want. That's it. Nothing else.

So who the hell would ever be stupid enough to not only tie themselves to a man like me but stick around as well?

That's the question that leaves me scratching my tattooed head over the next few days.

CHAPTER TWO

Kira

"Mr. Kozlov is very unhappy with you, Yury," Zeno says to my trembling father as he towers over him in our living room.

"The fire...it wasn't my fault," my father says before he breaks into his native Russian tongue.

After being raised in the home of two Russian immigrants for all of my twenty-three years, you would think I would've picked up the language by now.

I haven't. All I know are a few swear words.

My parents spoke English before they came to South Carolina and started their furniture business thirty years ago. Growing up, they spoke English ninety-nine percent of the time because they wanted me to fit in with all the other children in school. The only time I heard Russian was if my dad slammed the hammer on his finger, or if there was a problem he was discussing with my mother and didn't want me to know the details. It was their secret language, and one I knew always meant trouble.

I'm well aware that neither of my parents are saints. Despite their flaws, they're good people who have worked hard to give me everything I wanted or needed growing up. I only wish that my father's business wasn't tangled up with a criminal enterprise.

They may not have ever told me all the specifics, but I have figured out that hearing the name Boris Kozlov is enough to send my father into the bottom of a liquor bottle and my mother to church.

It's my belief that Kozlov is one of the heads of the Russian mafia. He must control his empire from his home country since I've never seen him. Instead of making personal visits, he sends goons like Zeno to the States to keep his business ventures running smoothly. My father receives imports from Russia, and since he's always kept me away from the docks and inventory, I don't see what comes in. I'm guessing it's more than wood and fabric...

"You owe Mr. Kozlov half a million for the lost merchandise," Zeno responds in English to my father.

Oh shit.

My parents were struggling to keep their heads above water *before* the fire in their warehouse wiped out all of their inventory. I've seen their bank statements, so I know they only have enough money to cover the bills for maybe two more months thanks to the fucking Russians taking a percentage of everything they earn.

"I'll have it for him soon," my father tells Zeno. "I'm just waiting for the insurance check."

Wait, what?

I know for a fact that the insurance check for the fire is only a little more than three-hundred grand for the structure and the inventory inside. If he gives it to this jackass for drugs or whatever illegal shit my father was storing for him, how will they afford to rebuild?

"You're running out of time. I'll be back for the check at the end of the week," Zeno responds. Placing his hands on his hips to open his suit jacket and reveal the guns on either side of his shoulder holster, he says, "If you don't have it by then, your wife will be cashing in your life insurance plan to reimburse Mr. Kozlov."

With that final threat on my father's life, the giant, bald meathead turns and leaves our house, causing my mother to softly utter a prayer in Russian.

"If you give him the insurance money, then how will you be able to afford another warehouse or-or pay the bills while you build all new inventory?" I ask my father since his craft takes time and dedication. He doesn't just slap a few pieces of wood together and call it good. He's a perfectionist, and he makes beautiful pieces of furniture.

"We won't," he responds, tugging on the corners of his graying mustache.

"What does that mean?" I ask.

"Your mother and I will just have to find other work," he huffs before softly adding, "And sell the house."

"Other work? There is no other work! You make furniture and she helps you sell it. Neither of you have any other skills!" I exclaim. "And you can't sell the house. Where will we live?"

"Don't worry, Kira. We'll figure it out," my father says. Pointing his index finger at me, he says, "You *will* go to school in the fall. No more putting it off!"

"How can I possibly leave you now of all times when everything is going to hell?" I ask him as tears blur my vision.

"You can and you will because I said so!" he shouts as he gets to his feet. Stomping over to the door, he rips his coat off the hook and says, "I'll be back before dinner, *моя любовь*," before he disappears.

"Mama, you're not gonna let him give in to those assholes, are you?" I ask when she gets up from the sofa and I follow her into the kitchen.

"What choice do we have? You heard the man. If we don't come up with the rest of the money and fast, he'll kill your father! Those threats are not idle."

"There has to be some other way for you to make Kozlov happy and rebuild the warehouse without selling the house," I tell her.

"No, Kira. There is not!" she responds with her back to me as she pulls out pots and pans from the lower cabinet. They clatter nosily because she's angry at me or my father or Kozlov, so she's banging them around on purpose. "Now, go! I have dinner to cook."

After she scolds me like I'm still a child, I take the hint that she wants to be alone and climb the stairs up to my bedroom. My entire life my parents have spoiled me, putting my happiness over theirs. They spent a ton of time and money they didn't have taking me to ballet classes for ten years, and they never missed a single one of my volleyball games in high school. After I was born, they started saving money to send me to pretty much any college I want to attend.

Five years after graduating from high school and I still haven't picked one. And each year since I've had to discreetly withdraw a little more money from my college fund to deposit into their account. I don't mind. The money is theirs, not mine. If I really wanted to go to college, I would have done so already, and I could probably get a student loan to cover tuition. The problem is that I still don't know what I want to even study. And how could I leave, knowing that son of a bitch Kozlov is making my parents' lives hell?

It's not fair. A man across the entire freaking ocean shouldn't be able to take the money my parents need.

There has to be some other way for us to get the money to rebuild. Maybe they could get a business loan.

One online application with a bank later entering in my parents' information and I'm disappointed to find out that's not an option thanks to their plummeting credit history. They must have been using credit cards to pay for supplies and didn't tell me, which means things are even worse than I thought.

I have to come up with a plan to help them get through this instead of letting some Russian bully win.

Typing in a quick search online of how to make hundreds of thousands of dollars fast isn't very helpful. We don't have anything of value to sell other than our home. I refuse to gamble away what little money is left in my college fund in a casino to try and make more.

Organ donation is extremely risky health wise, and illegal. Besides, it doesn't even pay that well!

I keep scrolling through the results pages until I find an article about how a woman sold her virginity online for a million dollars...

My virginity may be long gone, lost to Steve Baker in the back of his mom's station wagon after our senior prom, but it does give me another idea.

Thirty years ago, my parents had an arranged marriage of sorts in Russia, and it worked out well for them. My father was getting ready to come to the United States to start up his business; and my mother, who he randomly met and started talking to in the grocery store checkout line, wanted to leave the country and come with him for a better life. Her parents wouldn't let her leave with a man she just met, so they got married before coming over. They may not have started out loving each other, but they do now, that I'm certain of.

Aren't there old, rich men out in the world who are willing to pay for female companionship? I'm not looking for a million, but maybe half of that so that my parents can keep their home?

An internet search for mail-order brides brings up several results, including a few that are specifically Russian and Ukrainian.

Am I actually willing to enter into a marriage with someone I don't know for money, giving up the chance of finding love and marrying the man of my dreams?

Yes, I am, if it means making sure my parents will be okay. I would endure hell for them. They would do no less for me, so now it's time for me to repay the favor.

CHAPTER THREE

Miles

I'T'S HARD TO BELIEVE, but porn is my new way of life.

I'm a Savage fucking King, and lately, I'm the only person who touches my dick.

A few years ago, the clubhouse would be full of honeys looking to get laid by a big bad biker. And yeah, I know I'm not the hottest or most charismatic King. I still got a ton of ass from my brothers' leftovers, so that was fine by me. It was hard to find a woman to come back for seconds after getting my rough treatment, but there were plenty of women on rotation.

Now, everyone is getting married and having babies, so going upstairs to get my dick sucked is no longer happening. Most of the club girls are gone, and the ones left won't touch me right now because of how fucked up my face is after Reece's recent beating. It was his own damn fault for not telling me Cynthia was off limits and that he had a thing for her.

So, I'm not looking for much. I just want a sexy body warming my bed every once in a while. I know full well that I'm not the type of man women marry. Who could ever love a murderer like me? Not that I think I'm actually capable of loving anyone back...

Which leaves me with...porn.

And god, I hate watching porn, but I'm not desperate enough to drag my ass into a nasty whore house.

The women in these flicks are all fake as fuck. Even if they weren't, watching some other asshole screwing their brains out is nowhere close to being as good as being the one doing the screwing.

Porn also makes me sad. Sad because I'm so lonely and horny that I have to tug on my own cock while watching other people fuck.

Still, I have needs and a swollen shaft that occasionally needs some relief, so here I am, searching the internet for naked chicks sucking dick. Or I was, until a little box pops up on the screen.

An animated girl in a tiny black bikini wants to know if I'm a hard-working man looking for a submissive woman to cater to my every need.

Why, hell yes, I am.

I click on the big red button, and it takes me to a site that says something about mail-order brides from Russia.

Ooh, and I need to click now for an optimized experience, including a naughty private strip show from my potential bride.

Fuck yes.

I click on the link; then wait for the page to load.

Instead of a hot half-naked woman, I get a close up of an angry and familiar man's face, completely killing my mood.

"Reece?" I ask, squinting at the screen. "Why is your fat head on my screen? What the fuck are you doing?"

"What the fuck am I doing?" he asks. "I'm saving your ass! How in the hell did you manage to fuck up your computer this badly?"

"I was just...I mean, I was looking for some porn, you know..." I start and trail off thanks to his glare. The guy already hates my guts and tried to beat the shit out of me twice in one night. I don't need to go another round.

"Is there some reason you had to look at Russian porn?" he snaps at me. "What did you click on?"

"I thought I was getting set up for a private show, but I...shit, Reece, what happened?" I ask.

"You gave whoever is running this site administrative privileges. Did you see someone else moving your cursor around the screen, like I'm doing now?"

"Yeah, but they said they were just 'optimizing the experience'!"

"Goddammit, Miles," he sighs. "From now on, warn me whenever you get on one of your computers. You let some Russian hack bypass our VPN and get access to our servers."

"I...I don't know what that means," I admit. "Is it bad?"

"Yes, it's bad!" he shouts at me. "You allowed an outsider to access everything! All the club's records, you understand?"

"Oh shit, Reece, oh shit, can you fix it?" I ask as I try to get closer to see what he's doing.

"It's all right. Whoever you gave access to wasn't looking for anything specific, they started trying to copy our entire server. Since they were accessing us, I could access them too. I uploaded a program to them that I just launched. We're fine, now. But you bring that laptop to me right now, you hear me?" Reece yells at me.

I try to click around and find the page with the mail-order shit again, but it's no longer there.

Getting up, and glad I hadn't gotten to the part where I unzip my pants yet, I unplug the laptop and go knock on Reece's closed door.

My head hangs in embarrassment when he opens up. "Man, I'm sorry. I was just having a little fun looking at that website. It wasn't there anymore after you did...whatever you did. Is there any safe way I could check it out, you think?"

"There are plenty of safe ways to check out other websites," Reece replies. "It will probably be awhile before you see that one again, though. The program I uploaded and launched on their server wiped everything they tried to copy from us, and then formatted all their drives. I don't know what they were doing over there, but I shut that shit down."

"Oh, okay then," I respond, disappointed. "I guess I'll go shoot some pool or play cards with the boys. You want to come up for a while?" I ask, trying to repair the riff between us thanks to Cynthia.

"No," Reece snaps. "You managed to fuck up my night with this stunt, and I'm not in the mood for your companionship. Get out of my room."

"Grumpy bastard," I snort before shutting his door behind me on the way out.

Instead of going upstairs, I decide to go get another laptop from the chapel, playing it safer this time by not searching "dirty sluts sucking cock" and instead typing in "mail-order brides" to find out what that shit is all about.

And boom, there are a ton of sites offering women of all nationalities for marriage. One even has an option to check the little boxes for everything you're looking for in your dream wife. It all seems too good to be true.

Is finding a wife really as easy as clicking on a few buttons and paying a little cash?

It has to be easier than the traditional method. I'll be old and dead waiting for some knockout to show up at the bar and say she wants to sleep with me every night for the rest of my life.

Hell, forget forever, I would be happy keeping a woman around for a year since the club girls don't seem to want more than a few nights at most from me.

So, what do I have to lose if I buy myself a wife? I have plenty of money. The Kings do well with our various business enterprises, most of them even legally. Since I live at the clubhouse for free, I barely spend any of my earnings, which total nearly a million now. If I could find a woman who is desperate enough to marry me for some cash, then I could probably keep her around by just buying her nice shit or whatever. That seemed to always work on my mom with her husbands since she's never worked a day in her life.

There's no reason not to take a look around, see who is available on the site. So, I start going through the various criteria.

I definitely want her to speak English because I'll be damned if I'm smart enough to learn some other fucked-up language. Next, I select for her age to be under thirty. And finally, for the price, I select under half a million. I may have plenty of cash, but I'm not stupid enough to blow it all in one day on a woman I've never met.

Finished with my selections, I hit the enter button and I'm provided with three choices of equally beautiful women. Two of them are still over in the fucking Ukraine, so I'm not taking any chances on them lying about the English thing and then not being able to communicate, or even worse, getting deported. So that leaves...one girl – Kira. She's a twenty-three-year-old from down in Charleston, South Carolina.

No shit?

That's just a few hours away!

And Kira is...fucking gorgeous with long, straight, brown hair, the bluest shade of eyes, and big, plump cock-sucking lips. She's a steal at five-hundred thousand too.

I quickly read through the information on the site and determine that, in order to talk to the girl to work out the details of our contract, I have to create an account and then pay a non-refundable fee of one thousand dollars. But that once I pay up, she won't be able to accept any other offers unless our deal falls through.

I pull out my credit card from my wallet because that sounds fucking awesome to me.

CHAPTER FOUR

Kira

HOLY CRAP! I've got an email about a potential offer and my profile hasn't even been up for an hour!

Now I just have to log back into the site to talk to the guy and figure out the details. Hopefully he's not too old or creepy and he can come up with the money fast, like before Friday.

Once I'm logged in, I see the flashing envelope icon notification on the top of the page, indicating a new message. It's from member SavageKing69 and he's... asking me for nudes.

Great.

The guy could be some random pervert, but he must have paid a thousand dollars that he won't get back even if this falls through in order to send that message.

There's also a little green dot by his user name, indicating that he's still online.

I type back to him, **"How do I know you're serious**

about going through with this? Do you really have half a million dollars, or are you stupid enough to pay a thousand dollars to try and get a nude pic?"

His response comes back a few seconds later, **"Dead serious but need to see the goods before I buy. Half a million is a lot of damn money. It'd be a waste to spend it on a flat-chested chick and have to pay for implants. Show me what you're working with, princess."**

Wow. The man is certainly...blunt, that's for sure. I've never done anything like this before, but I don't want to lose a potential buyer.

Getting up to go lock my bedroom door, I pull my shirt over my head on the way back to my computer desk, and then use my phone to take a photo. Even though I'm still wearing a bra, I make sure my face isn't visible in case the image ends up on the web. Then I upload and send the picture to SavageKing69.

His instant response is **"Very nice tits."**

Trying to prevent him from requesting any nude photos, I quickly get to work asking him his age and where he's from.

While I know it's impossible to choose, I hope I don't have to move all the way to the west coast since that will make it difficult for me to see my parents.

SavageKing69 tells me he's only thirty-four, which is surprising since I thought most rich guys on these sites were old and decrepit. It's a huge plus that he's not. And he says he lives in North Carolina!

"That's perfect," I type to him because it means I'll still be close enough to drive home to see my mom and dad.

"Are you able to finalize everything by Friday?" I ask, afraid this guy is too good to be true and I'm getting my hopes up.

"Hell yeah. The sooner the better," is his response.

"Great, then let's talk about what each of us want included in the contract," I type to him.

SavageKing69's response is one word, **"Sex."**

Of course. I figured the physical aspect would be brought up pretty fast since he wanted to see my breasts. I'm also aware of the fact that if a man pays that much money to marry me, he's going to want to sleep with me.

And I'm going to need some time to prepare myself for getting naked with a stranger. Four days isn't exactly long enough, though, so I'll need to come around to the idea or this whole mail-order bride idea is pointless.

Blowing out a breath, I try to figure out how to respond while keeping his interest and also being completely honest.

Finally, I tell him, **"I don't know you, and have never met you, so I can't promise that I'll have sex with you whenever you want. Anyone who agrees to that would be lying, so I'm not going to lie to you and say it's going to happen. But, I'm willing to give marriage a real shot, which includes intimacy, eventually."**

There. I left the door open to the possibility since it's the truth and I have to give some shred of hope to get the money and fast.

"I can work with that," SavageKing69 says which is a relief. Then he adds, **"As long as I get to have you on our wedding night."**

Oh shit.

"You want me to sleep with you the first day we meet?" I ask in horror. I have no idea what he looks like, if I'll be attracted to him, or repulsed!

"It's a fucking tradition," is his response.

I tell him, **"That's asking a lot."**

SavageKing69 says, **"So is demanding a man pay half a million damn dollars to marry you."**

"Touché," I type back with a smile on my face. Closing my eyes and scrubbing my palms over my face, I try to imagine the absolute worst man I can, then try to picture getting naked with him and letting him touch me.

19

It makes me feel incredibly nauseous.

But so does the image of my parents having to sell their house and work shitty jobs, or even worse, my father dead, murdered by the Russian assholes because he didn't get the money they say he owes by Friday.

Still, if I'm going to have to put out to make this deal happen, I need something in return.

"If we have sex on our wedding night, you lose all rights to a refund," I shoot back to SavageKing69.

"Half a refund," he quickly counters. **"I'm not paying two-hundred grand for a one-night stand."**

He makes a valid point. And my intention with this arranged marriage slash mail-order bride business wasn't to whore myself out. With two hundred and fifty thousand and the three-hundred thousand from insurance, my dad can pay back the Russians, assuming the check comes from the insurance company in time.

Sleeping with a man who is going to be my husband is a small price to pay to ensure my parents have the money in time.

"Deal," I agree. "**What else?**"

It feels like I have to wait half an hour for SavageKing69's next response, which is too long when time is running out for my father. Finally, he says, **"I want a guarantee that you won't immediately back out and get a divorce. You don't have to agree to be with me forever, but you can't take my money and run."**

"Understood," I reply because I'm not a complete bitch trying to screw the guy over.

"So, if you leave before a year is up, I get half my money back," he tells me.

One year living with a strange man to make sure my parents will be okay? That doesn't seem so bad. I can get through anything for one year. And this guy doesn't seem old or hateful, just a little pervy and blunt.

"Deal," I tell him.

"What do you want, Kira?" he asks, making my grin widen because he even bothered to ask and because he used my name.

"You can't hurt me," I type to him. **"If you physically assault me, I'll call the police. Our marriage will be over, and I get to keep all of the money."**

"Deal," he agrees, which is a relief. **"I won't hurt you, and I won't let anyone else hurt you either."**

Wow. That's sort of sweet.

"Good, then that's all for me. Anything else for you?" I reply.

"Do you want kids?"

I take a second to think that one over before I respond, not really sure why he wants to know. But I guess that, after people get married, they usually have kids. Some don't ever want them, though. It's probably a good thing to discuss before taking vows.

Did my parents ever imagine that they would have a happy marriage, including me when they made their arrangement? Probably not.

And I do want kids. Several would be nice because, growing up as an only child, I was lonely, even more so when there's no other sibling around to help me deal with the current mess my parents are in.

What if SavageKing69 doesn't want kids.

If I say yes, does it mean our deal is off?

I'm not going to lie, so eventually, I tell him, **"Yes, someday, and more than one."**

"Good. That's perfect," he tells me, which is a relief.

"Great," I agree. **"I'll have an attorney draft up the contract and send it to you tomorrow for you to sign. Will that work?"**

"I'll get the money ready," he responds.

I'm getting ready to end the chat when I realize I don't even know his first name. **"I'll need your full name for the contract. I'm guessing it's not SavageKing69."**

"It's Miles. Miles Taylor. You may want to start getting used to the last name."

Miles. I like it.

And Kira Taylor isn't all that bad either.

"Thanks, Miles," I say to the man who may have just unknowingly saved my father's life.

CHAPTER FIVE

Miles

I DON'T KNOW or understand but maybe half of the words in the goddamn marriage contract.

And while my cock is all for me agreeing and sending over half a million dollars to a beautiful woman I've never met with amazing tits, my head is concerned that this could be a huge mistake.

I need someone to read through all the legalese shit and tell me if I'm agreeing to my entire life savings or something first.

I guess I could ask Reece since he's really fucking smart, but he's still angry with me about the website hacking thing.

Sax is a brainiac too; but when I try to call him, his phone goes to voicemail.

Torin isn't around, and I don't really want Chase and Abe knowing my business and laughing it up.

Guess my next stop is the short walk over to Avalon to see Cooper. The former military man manages a club, so he's sharp as a tack. I bet he even deals with contracts or whatever with the strippers. And the scenery doesn't exactly hurt either. Seeing Coop means seeing tits, which is just fine with me.

"What's up?" Cooper asks after a quick glance up at me before he goes back to whatever work he's doing on the laptop on the desk in his office.

"Why don't you sit in the main room and watch tits all day?" I ask him curiously.

"That shit gets old fast," he says, but I refuse to believe such a thing is true. It's the equivalent of saying a man can have too much sex. "And I actually have shit to do that requires peace and quiet. What do you need?"

"I, ah, I've got a contract I need someone to read before I sign it."

"A contract for what?" he asks.

"Ugh, here, just read it," I say, going over to toss the paperwork down in front of him.

He picks it up, and his eyes skim the first page for about ten seconds before he looks at me over the top. "You're buying a woman?"

"A wife, yeah. And you can't tell any fucking body!" I warn him.

"Why?"

"Because I don't want everyone knowing my business."

"No, man," Coop says with a sigh. "Why the hell are you buying a woman?"

"Why not?" I reply with a shrug of my shoulders.

"You got me there," he responds with a shake of his head and a grin before he keeps reading. Finally done with all the pages, he offers the stack back to me and says, "Look, man, I don't even know some of that legal jargon. You probably need an attorney to give you the okay."

"An attorney? Yeah," I agree. "You know any?"

"Ah, I know one, sure," he responds and tugs at the collar of his dress shirt. Looking up at the clock on the wall, he says, "It's lunchtime, so Liz is probably in her office if you want to try and stop by."

"Who?" I ask.

"Elizabeth Townsend," he replies. "She's one of the MC's criminal defense attorneys, but I think she would help you out with the contract as a favor to me."

"Yeah, that sounds good, the sooner the better."

"Okay," he agrees, getting to his feet. Grabbing his Savage King cut from the back of his chair, he slips his arms into it and says, "Follow me. And try not to act a fool."

"I'll try my best," I agree with a snicker.

THE ATTORNEY's office is over in Beaufort, on the mainland, so it's a short drive over the bridge.

We park in the lot of a five-story building, one that's fancy on the inside and has a list of about thirty names of businesses and people in the building.

"Liz is on the fifth floor," Cooper says when he presses the button to call the elevator.

There's Kenny G or some shit playing over the speakers in the elevator. The interior is made up entirely of mirrors; and even though we're the only ones inside, the reflections keep startling me.

Cooper leads the way off the elevator down to the end of the hall where he opens a door and walks into a small waiting room that's empty.

"Hey, Barb. Is Liz in?" Coop asks at the receptionist window.

Smiling up at Cooper like he's a movie star, the blonde woman picks up the phone. "Mr. Cummings is here to see you," she says before hanging up and telling Coop, "She said you can come on back."

"Great, thanks," he responds.

"Your last name is Cummings?" I exclaim followed by a chuckle. "How did I not know that?"

"Shut up," Coop says as we go through another door and down a narrow hall to the office in the back-left corner. He raps his knuckles quickly on the door before turning the handle and walking on in.

Inside the office, a short, curvy blonde stands up from behind her enormous desk covered in accordion files and starts unbuttoning the top of her blue blouse, her eyes lowered to focus on her task. "We'll have to make this quick. I have to be in court in an hour..." she starts and then finally looks up. "Oh, so I guess it's not *that* kind of appointment. Unless you're planning on having your friend join us?" she asks, head high and without missing a beat or even blushing.

"Hell no," Cooper snaps at the same time I say, "Hell fucking yes."

Coop shoots me a glare before he tells her, "We're here on business. Can you look over a contract?"

If he says today is business, then I'm guessing Coop's *other* visits must be strictly for pleasure. Now it makes sense why he calls her Liz like they're good buddies. Fuck buddies, if I had to guess.

"Sure," the small but fiercely confident woman agrees, reaching her hand out.

"This is my friend, Miles," Cooper says. "Miles Taylor, this is Elizabeth Townsend."

"One of your brother's in arms apparently," Elizabeth remarks as she looks between us and our identical leather cuts then stares at the skull tat that wraps around my throat.

I hand her the paperwork, and she puts on a pair of thin glasses, then leans over the desk to read while standing, giving me a peek at her heavy tits spilling out the top of her white lace bra. I barely get to enjoy it before Coop steps in front of me, blocking the view.

After a few seconds, she looks up and asks me around his body, "Have you met her?"

"Ah, sort of," I respond. "I've seen her picture and we've talked online."

"You're paying to marry a woman without even meeting her first. That's risky..."

"Can he even do that?" Coop asks the lawyer.

"Yes," she agrees before she flips to the next page.

Since it's going to take a while, I walk around the room, coming to a stop at the statue of a blind-folded woman holding scales in one hand and a sword in another. The scales even move when I put my finger on it.

"Keep your hands to yourself," Coop mutters from behind me. "What are you, five?"

"Plus or minus thirty years," I joke.

"Well," Elizabeth starts, "legally, as long as this contract lays out everything you both agreed to, then I don't see any problems with it. Basically, it's no different than a prenup. Do you need a prenup?"

"Nah, most of my money is in a fireproof safe that requires my fingerprint," I tell her.

"All right then," she says, handing the stack back to me. "Looks like you're all set. Congrats, I guess."

"Great," I say in relief. "You got one of those canaries around for me to sign it and stamp it?" I ask her.

"Ah, sure," Elizabeth replies with a grin. "Beth, our secretary, is a *notary*, so she can do that if you have a photo ID," she says before pushing a button on the phone and asking the woman to come to her office with her notary stamp. Once that's taken care of, she turns back to me and says, "You do know that even if you're married, you'll still need her consent to...whenever you want to..."

"To what?" I ask.

"Oh, Jesus," Coop mutters, rubbing his fingers over his temples. "To fuck her, man, to fuck her! Marriage doesn't mean you can hit it whenever you want."

"Yeah, I know that," I huff. Kira came right out and said she wouldn't agree to screw me whenever I say the word. But she did agree to it the night we get married, and then to try and make this a real marriage after that.

And I mean, how hard could it be to convince a woman who lives with me and sleeps in my bed to spread her legs once in a while for me?

Oh fuck.

I can't expect my wife to live in my shitty little apartment at the clubhouse. It smells like cigars, stale pizza and booze with a hint of sweat and cum. A woman as beautiful as Kira deserves better.

"Is there anything else I can help you gentlemen with today?" Elizabeth asks.

"Ah, yeah," I answer. "Who do I need to talk to about buying a house?"

CHAPTER SIX

Kira

"Mom, Dad, we need to talk," I say to my parents after we finish dinner and are all still sitting at our dining table.

"What is it, *маленький*?" my father asks, still calling me "little one" even though I'm twenty-three.

"I have some news."

"Have you finally decided on a college?" he asks, face brightening with a grin. Shit. He's going to be so disappointed when I tell him what I plan to do, and he realizes I may *never* go to college like he always wanted for me.

"No, ah, not yet," I say. "But I am leaving home soon."

"What do you mean you're leaving home?" my mother asks. "Where are you going if not to school?"

"I'm, uh, I'm getting married."

My mother and father look at each other in confusion before my dad finally speaks again. "What?" he simply asks.

"I'm getting married. There's a man in North Carolina, and I've agreed to meet him Friday at a little chapel by the sea."

My father rapidly fires questions at me. "Who is this man? How do you know him? What is the rush, Kira?"

"Okay, so don't freak out, but it's sort of an arranged marriage, like yours. He's going to give me some money, so you won't have to sell the house. Think of it as an old school dowry."

"Kira, honey, are you feeling okay?" my mother asks, and even reaches over to put her palm on my forehead as if checking my temperature.

"I'm fine and I've already made this decision so you can't try to talk me out of it. The contract has been signed and the money will be wired into your bank account on Friday after the ceremony. I'm telling you now because I hope that you'll come with me, that daddy will walk me down the aisle."

"We've never met the man. Have you? This is absurd," my father says. "Let me see this ridiculous contract!"

"Why is it so absurd? You and mom had an arranged marriage. Did you meet her father before the wedding? Before you two decided to get married and leave the country with her to live thousands of miles away?"

"No, but..." he starts.

"Then you don't get to be angry at me for this!" I tell him. "I'm doing it because you and mom gave me everything growing up. It's the least I can do for you."

"No!" my father exclaims. "We don't need you to take care of us. We're the parents and you're the child! We are supposed to take care of you, not the other way around," he says before he gets to his feet and launches into various Russian curses.

"Kira," my mom starts, reaching for my hand and covering it with hers. "You don't have to do this. I'm sure you can tell them you changed your mind."

"No, I'm not changing my mind. It's done. So, are you going to help me pick out a wedding dress, or am I going to have to go do that on my own?" I ask.

Tears fill my mother's tired, blue eyes as she stares silently at me. "I'll go. Of course, I'll go if you're certain this is what you want."

"Good," I reply in relief.

I had several close friends in high school, but they've all moved on, gone to college and gotten married themselves, so my mom is my best friend. She's always been there for me so I can't imagine doing this, getting married, without her help. "And will you come to the wedding too?" I ask.

"It'll break my heart, but I'll be there," she says as the tears start to race down each of her cheeks.

"No, this is a good thing. He's a nice man, and who knows? I may fall in love with him like you fell in love with daddy."

"Right, yes," she agrees with a nod as she grabs a napkin to dab over her eyes, but I can still hear the doubt in her voice.

"Daddy?" I ask when he continues pacing around the dining room, refusing to speak to me in English. I catch bits and pieces, pretty sure that he says something about *hating that bastard Kozlov.*

"Daddy, will you walk me down the aisle or not?" I say when he continues to ignore me.

"Yes, dammit, yes!" he shouts before he says something in Russian to my mother and then leaves the room. I hear the front door slam a few seconds later.

"What did he say?" I ask her.

"He said he's sorry that you were born as stubborn as I am," she tells me with a sad smile.

"It's going to be okay, Mama," I assure her. "Trust me."

"I hope you're right, Kira," she replies. "Because marriage is not something to be taken lightly. Your grandparents, they will disown you if you divorce him."

"Wait, what?" I ask her. "I haven't seen them in years anyway. Why would they care if I get married or divorced?"

"They care. It's why I stayed with your father even when he

drove me crazy those first few years! Now I'm glad I stayed, I am. But it wasn't always easy."

"Try not to worry, Mama," I tell her. "Let's just hope for the best."

"Standing up and making a promise to a man in front of God is not something you can take lightly or hope for the best! It's a lifetime commitment, not some arrangement to be made for money that you can take back whenever you want! When you marry him, the two of you will become one spirit, one flesh, and that union doesn't end even in death. The Orthodox tradition doesn't condone divorce. Nor does it allow a widow to remarry. Loving anyone but your husband is forbidden!"

"I won't take it back, okay? I'll...I'll stay with him forever," I say, even though the words make me feel dizzy and feverish as that reality sinks in.

One man forever.

Never falling in love with anyone for the rest of my life, other than my husband.

What if I can't love him?

Even though they're my mother and grandparents' beliefs and not mine, if I get a divorce, it will kill my mother and her family to think I'm damned for all eternity. And I will *never* tell them I'm not a virgin on my wedding night.

But the marriage is public, so there's no hiding it. I'll just have to make this work with Miles no matter what.

Even if he's a hideous monster or an evil man.

"Forever, yes," my mother says with a nod. "If you still want to do this, then I guess we'll have to find you the perfect dress, one to make him fall in love with you at first sight and never long for another woman."

CHAPTER SEVEN

Miles

"You busy this afternoon?" I ask Cooper when I burst into his office Friday at lunchtime.

"Ah, just working here like usual."

"Can you spare half an hour or so out?"

"Maybe. Why?" he asks.

"Because I'm getting married," I respond.

"No shit? Already?" he says with a grin. "You're really going to go through with this?"

"Yeah. I even bought a house and all too."

"Seriously? Damn, that was fast. Are you inviting the other Kings to the ceremony?" he asks.

"No. Just you. I want someone there, but I don't need shit from all them about this," I explain. "You haven't told anyone, have you?"

"Nope. Not a soul," he says. "And Liz won't either. Attorney-client privilege and all that."

"So, you and Liz are hooking up, huh?" I ask him. "You have a building full of naked women and you're fucking the lawyer?"

"How about you mind your own damn business and worry about the woman you've never met?" he huffs. "What if she robs you blind?"

"She can't," I tell him. "My fingerprint is the only one that opens the safe."

"She could cut it off in your sleep," he responds with a smile. "Or cut off your cock while you're asleep, wait for you to bleed out, and then cut off your finger."

My jaw drops as that visual sinks in. When I recover, I tell him, "Wow, thanks for putting that fucked-up worry in my head!"

"Look, man, you never know how crazy a woman is until you live with her."

"How many women have you lived with?" I ask him.

"I pretty much live with ten in here, all day, every day," he explains. "And these women who work for dollar bills? They are the most vicious. I have to keep an eye out for heroin and cocaine. Don't even get me started on how many have been arrested for beating up other women out in public or their boyfriends..."

"They really do that?" I ask.

"Hell yes," he responds. "That's what I'm trying to tell you! You don't know anything about this woman you're paying a shit ton of money to marry. She could have a psycho boyfriend who could come after you. Did you think about that?"

"I can take care of myself," I assure him. Pushing the sides of my cut back, I lift up my gray t-shirt, revealing the ever-growing flock of black birds, each one representing a life I personally took from this earth. "Thirty-nine confirmed fucking kills as a Marine and civilian."

"Yeah, I know," Coop says, looking a little pale at the running tally on the side of my body. "But those were all men. Women can fuck you over, and there's nothing you can do about it."

"My mom's been married six times, taking everything from every man who divorces her, including his dignity and self-respect, so I'm well aware of how the other half works," I tell him.

"I'm just trying to look out for you, man," Cooper says. "I hope this marriage shit works out for you, really I do. The odds just aren't in your favor."

"Well, I'm still doing this today, so are you coming or not?" I ask him, pissed that he's ruining this for me before it even starts.

"I'll be there," he says. "Can't wait to see the poor girl you suckered into marrying you," he jokes with a grin.

"Yeah, me too," I agree with a grin. "Oh, and do you know where I can find some rings fast?"

"Lord help you both," he mutters with a shake of his head.

Kira

THE NERVES DON'T REALLY HIT me until we pull up at the tiny chapel, me in my Honda packed with my clothes and other belongings and my parents in their old beat-up Buick with disappointment written all over their faces.

I try to put on a smile when I get out of my car even when the voice in my head keeps repeating over and over again, "You're getting married today," as I reach for the dress bag in the back seat.

I'm getting ready to marry a man I've never seen before.

And at first, I thought that was sort of sad for him. Now the worst possible scenarios are going through my mind.

He could've lied about his age and he's actually eighty-five.

Or what if he weighs like five-hundred pounds and rarely leaves the house so that's why he wants a wife, to take care of him?

Or what if he's just ugly and weird looking?

Those things are starting to matter more now that the day is here.

Tonight, I have to go to bed with whoever is waiting at the end of the aisle no matter how disgusting they are!

What was I thinking, agreeing to something so insane?

Maybe my parents are right, and I can still back out.

My parents.

That's why I'm doing this. That's the reason I will *not* back out or ask for a divorce no matter how much I may want one. We need the money to keep my father alive, and it's the only way.

It's just one time.

One. Time.

I can do anything once.

After I sleep with him tonight, I won't have to touch the man who bought me to be his wife again, and my parents will both be alive and happy.

And so what if I have to live with him for at least a year and can never get divorced? A year is a short amount of time in the big scheme of things. Being miserable for three-hundred and sixty-five days is worth the price of my mother and father's happiness.

Isn't it?

Yes. Of course it is. Any daughter would make this same sacrifice. So I need to suck it up, blink away tears, and put on my big girl panties along with my wedding dress.

"Come on. I need to get changed," I tell my mom as I grab her arm and pull her up the steps of the chapel.

"What am I supposed to do?" my father asks.

"Just...wait here," I tell him. "Once I'm dressed, I'll come back out and wait here with you until they're ready to start."

"You sure this is the right place?" my mother asks when I push open the door into the dusty chapel that sits on the dunes, the beach within sight along with its familiar salty scent, reminding me of home.

"Ah, yeah, it's the right place," I reply. "Hello? Is anyone here?" I call out.

About that time, a guy comes out of the men's restroom off to the right of the vestibule. He's handsome, with ear-length dirty-blond hair. He doesn't look dressed for a wedding, although he is wearing a black leather vest with a white dress shirt underneath and black slacks.

Could he be Miles?

"Oh shit," he says, eyes widening when he looks me up and down and then glances at my mother before his eyes come back to me. "You're her? You're the girl marrying Miles?"

So, he's not my husband. I'm a little disappointed since he's not old or ugly.

"That's me," I say. "I'm Kira," I tell him, transferring the dress back to my left arm to offer him my right hand.

He shakes it, his mouth opening and closing as if trying to figure out what to say, my cheeks reddening the entire time he stares at me. "Cooper. I'm Cooper. Miles is my, um, friend, my brother," he finally manages.

"Nice to meet you," I tell him. "I guess I should get changed?" I ask, nodding to the women's restroom over on the right.

"Yeah," he says. "I'll let Miles know you're here."

"Great, thanks," I tell him, barely refraining from asking what my soon-to-be husband looks like.

Just as I turn and start to push open the door with my mother behind me, Cooper asks, "Could you please try not to chop off any of Miles' body parts while he's sleeping? Or awake?"

My mother gasps at the random question.

Glancing over my shoulder at him, I say, "I wasn't planning on it."

"Good," he says with an exhale of relief. And I think it's kind of adorable how protective he is of his brother. But then he goes on to add, "Cause you seem like a nice girl and I would hate for anything bad to happen to you."

"Oh, okay. Thanks," I say as my face falls in understanding.

He's worried about *me* getting hurt, not Miles, which concerning considering I'm about to become his wife.

CHAPTER EIGHT

Miles

"She's here," Coop says when I walk out of the bathroom. "You just missed her. She's changing."

"Really? What's she like?" I ask.

"Young and sort of shy and...beautiful," he says with a sigh. "Are you sure you want to do this to her? Kira seems like a nice girl."

Gritting my teeth and getting in his face, I tell him, "I'm not making her do anything!"

"Right, she agreed to this for a big stack of cash, I get that," Coop huffs. "But don't you think you're rushing into something that could end badly? Why couldn't the two of you try dating or whatever for a little while?"

"Because I don't fucking date!" I shout at him. "Now shut the hell up or leave because I'm tired of you running your mouth. I *never* should've come to you about any of this. So much for being *brothers*."

As I'm walking away toward the front of the church to find the minister, Cooper grabs my elbow to stop me.

"I'm sorry, okay? I just don't understand your thought process here. You've always been a little...impulsive. But if you're sure this is what you want to do, then I'll stay. Someone should be here for you." He lets go of my elbow to shove a palm against my chest. "You're getting fucking married, man."

"Yeah, I am. And there's nothing you or anyone else can say to change my –"

Our conversation is interrupted when the chapel door opens, bathing us in sunlight. A tall, lean man with salt and pepper hair and a mustache comes wandering in wearing a navy-blue suit.

"Are you Kira's father?" Cooper asks him.

"Yes, I am," he replies with a hint of an accent I can't place.

"Don't worry," Coop says. "If Miles hurts her, I'll kill him for you."

"I'm not gonna hurt her!" I exclaim.

The concern on her father's scrunched face says he's not convinced.

"If I could talk my daughter out of this, I would," the man says. "My wife's father didn't have any luck convincing her to change her mind about me, a man she had just met in the supermarket when I told her I was leaving soon for the United States. Now we've been married for thirty wonderful years."

"Is that right?" Cooper asks in surprise.

"I'm not just worried about him hurting her," the man says, eyeing me. "I'm also sad because of the reason she's doing it."

"Why is that?" I ask, but I don't hear his response, or if he even gives one when the most gorgeous woman I've ever seen suddenly appears behind him. She looks like a princess with her caramel hair pulled up except for a few loose pieces that trail down her slender neck. The tight ivory dress shows off her perfect hourglass figure and is embroidered with flowers that sweep to the floor. My favorite part may be the thin straps hanging off her shoulders, looking like they're begging to be yanked down to release her beautiful round tits that I've already seen and fallen in love with.

Fuck, Kira's even sexier in person, and I can't wait to get that white pristine gown dirty tonight.

Dammit.

I didn't ask her if she was a virgin. God, I really hope not. If so, she'll go running as soon as I touch her. I don't do gentle.

Even if she's not a virgin, I can tell by the look in her wide blue eyes that she's already scared of me.

But I don't mind that at all. The fear will make fucking her even better when she finally submits. And she will, no matter how long it takes.

She's all mine now.

Tonight, I'll fuck her so good that she'll be begging me for more, and I'll gladly give it to her whenever she wants.

Hopefully.

"Are we ready to start?" the minister asks when he appears at the altar.

"Hell yes," I answer gruffly before Coop clasps a hand on my shoulder to drag me backward to the front of the church.

Kira

I GLANCE around the chapel and even behind me looking for the unfortunate man I'm supposed to marry. There's no one else here except for my parents, Cooper, an older man in a black suit holding a Bible, who I assume is the minister, and a tall, tough looking guy with a muscular body. A sleeve of angry yet bad boy sexy tattoos cover his entire left arm and massive biceps. Even his throat and the sides of his shaved head have inked designs. Like his brother, he's also wearing a black leather biker vest with white patches, a plain gray tee underneath and well-worn denim jeans. And his dark, intimidating gaze is fixated on me. I don't think he's looked away or blinked since I walked out.

Wow, he's...intense.

That can't be Miles, can it?

It must be, even if it doesn't make sense.

He's hot in a dangerous, almost villainous way thanks to the black facial hair that lines his jaw.

And he's nothing like I expected.

Surely, he can find women without having to pay one to marry him.

Although, there is a certain look in his dark eyes that makes me think he enjoys hurting people.

Please don't let him hurt me, I pray to a god I'm not even sure I believe in.

"Are we waiting on anyone else?" the minister asks from where he's waiting at the altar.

"No," the man who has to be Miles answers, eyes still locked on mine, holding me hostage.

"Right. Well, if there's no music, then we'll get right to it," he replies.

My father's face appears in front of me, blocking the strange and somewhat frightening man I'm about to marry from my line of sight and breaking the hypnosis he put me under. "Are you absolutely sure about this?" he asks.

"Y-yes," I stammer.

His response is in Russian, but still he turns around and loops his arm through mine to walk me down the aisle while my mother fusses with the train of my dress. As if it matters if it's crooked to the three other people in the room with us.

We come to a stop where the minister is waiting with Miles standing on his right and Cooper on the other side.

"Who gives this woman to this man?" the minister asks.

"Her father," my dad answers and then he takes my hand and offers it to Miles, who looks down at it for several seconds as if unsure what to do before finally taking it. His palm on mine is warm and calloused like he's worked hard in life. And also strong, like he has no plan to let me go anytime soon. I can't decide if that's comforting or worrisome.

"And so this bride and groom present themselves to be married today," the minister starts. "Marriage is a promise between two people who honor one another as individuals in that togetherness, and who wish to spend the rest of their lives together. It enables the two separate bodies and souls to become one, to share their desires, longings, dreams, and memories, their joys and sorrows, and to help each other through all uncertainties of life. A strong marriage also nurtures each of you as separate individuals and allows you to maintain your unique identity and grow in your own way through the years ahead. It is a safe haven for each of you to become your best self while together you become better than you ever could be alone."

It all sounds so romantic and yet nothing like it fits the circumstances today. If the minister wrote a truly accurate speech for us, he would say, *"This bride and groom present themselves today to be married because the bride had no other choice and the groom wants... who the hell knows what from her other than sex."*

I shake those thoughts out of my head and try my best to pretend that I know and care for the man who is holding my hand tightly while the loquacious minister continues his spiel.

"You are adding to your life not only the affection of each other, but also the companionship and blessing of a deep trust. To make this relationship work, though, it takes more than love."

Whew! That's a relief because there is no love.

"It takes trust, to know in your hearts that you want only the best for each other. It takes dedication, to stay open to one another, to learn and grow, even when it is difficult to do so. And it takes faith, to go forward together without knowing what the future holds for you both."

Now that part I can definitely agree with wholeheartedly. I have no clue what's in store for me tonight, since I agreed to let him inside me, or tomorrow morning when I wake up with a man I don't know but who is my husband.

"Kira, please repeat after me," the minister says. "I, Kira, take you Miles to be my husband."

Oh, shit, I'm supposed to speak now?

I repeat back the words, hoping I don't leave any out. The minister goes on, so I must be in the clear.

"I will share my life with you, build our dreams together, support you through times of trouble and rejoice with you in times of happiness," I echo before the final part. "I promise to give you respect, love and loyalty through all the trials and triumphs of our lives together."

"Wonderful," the minister says. "Now, Miles, repeat after me, I, Miles, take you Kira to be my wife."

I look up at Miles' serious and stern face as he struggles to remember all the words he's supposed to say to me, wondering what he's thinking about. Am I what he expected, or is he disappointed? He didn't cancel the wedding, so he must find me acceptable for half a million.

After we exchange white gold wedding bands provided by Cooper, then say "I do", I find out exactly what was on his mind.

The minister tells Miles he can now kiss his bride. Our deal has been made. It's done and over. My new husband leans forward to place his lips over my ear, and I almost gasp just from the unexpected placement of his kiss since it wasn't on my lips. But then he whispers to me, "You're so fucking sexy and now you're mine. I can't wait to ravage you tonight," stealing all the air from my lungs.

CHAPTER NINE

Miles

"I'll give you a minute to say goodbye to your folks," I tell Kira, now my wife, before I finally let her hand go and walk out of the church.

Even when I can no longer see her, there's this new, heavy weight on my finger where a wedding band now resides, like a constant physical reminder of the beautiful woman I'm tied to. I've never been a fan of jewelry before now, but I think I can get used to this one that gleams noticeably in the sunlight, knowing my wife has a matching ring that warns other men that she's taken. That she's *mine.*

I'm a lucky bastard. Seeing her in person makes it's easier than ever to pay up on my end of our deal. Ninety-nine percent of all my doubts about doing this have been erased.

A quick and easy call to the bank manager whose number I had on speed dial and the cash I deposited is being instantly wired to the account Kira listed on our agreement.

"Holy shit. You actually did it," Cooper says when he joins me outside. "No one is ever going to believe it..."

"You can't tell anyone," I spin around on the heels of my boots to remind him as I put away my phone in my cut.

"But you're married," he says with his brow furrowed. "I thought you were only keeping the pre-marriage details a secret."

"When I want other people to know, I'll fucking tell them," I explain.

Who knows how long Kira will actually stick around? Saying she's committing to at least a year is one thing, and actually doing it is another.

"Fine. Whatever, man," Coop says, holding up his palms in front of him. "I need to get back to Avalon before the night crowd starts rolling in. You good here?" he asks.

"Yeah, I'm good," I agree just as Kira and her parents come down the steps of the chapel. They both give her a hug and share a concerned look in my direction before getting in their car and driving away. Cooper is on his bike leaving right behind them.

Then it's just me and my wife standing in the sandy parking lot. She comes over to me but stops about ten feet away.

"That your ride?" I ask, nodding to the white Honda as I slip my sunglasses on over my eyes.

"Yeah."

"You gonna follow me to the house, or are you gonna make a run for it?"

"Leave before I sleep with you to get at least half the cash? Absolutely not," she says with a slight smile curving the corners of her full lips even though I can hear the tremor in her voice.

"Right," I reply. "Then let's get you out of that dress."

Her cheeks instantly flame a bright shade of red after my comment.

"You're not a virgin, are you?" I ask.

"No," she huffs as if she's insulted by the question.

"Good, I won't have to go easy on you," I reply. "Not that I could even if I wanted to."

Her sexy painted red lips part, but before she can change her mind about running, I tell her, "Let's go. I can at least drive slow this time so you can keep up."

"Ah, thanks," she says. She goes over and sits down in the front driver seat of her car. It takes her a few minutes to get all of her dress inside before the door shuts.

And I make a mental note to hide her car keys as soon we get to the house. No reason to make leaving easy for her.

Kira

"THE PLACE still needs a little work, but I got it for a steal," Miles says when he goes to unlock the door to the yellow house sitting on stilts. "The sound is just a block that way," he says, gesturing with his thumb over his shoulder. "And the ocean is four blocks on the other side."

"That's...nice," I say since my stomach is in knots. How can he talk to me so...casually when I'm a mess because of what we're about to do?

"I need to do some painting on the inside and out," he goes on to say when he pushes the door open and motions with his hand for me to go in first. Inside there are shiny, new, cherry wood floors with a black leather sofa and loveseat, a small square four-person dining table beside the kitchen that has all new stainless-steel appliances. Other than the furniture, the place is empty. There are no photographs on the wall or decorations of any kind. Not that Miles looks like the type of man to have decorations...

"I should, ah, I should probably bring my things up and unpack," I say to try and delay the inevitable a little longer.

"I'll get it all in for you," Miles replies. "*After*."

No further explanation is needed for the 'after' that he's referring to. From behind me, he reaches and takes the keyring from my hand.

The jingling sound disappears, like he tucked them into his pocket, then his hands come down on both of my shoulders. He tugs the sleeves of my dress down them even further until my breasts are nearly uncovered. "There's only one bed, so it shouldn't be hard to find," he informs me as his hands clasp my shoulders to guide me forward, down the short hall.

"You-you want to...right-right now?" I stammer.

"Oh yeah," he agrees, steering me into the bedroom with only a dresser and a big king size bed taking up the center of the floor. A solid black comforter removes any ideas of softness from the scene.

Spinning me around so that I'm facing him just inches away, Miles wets his lips with his tongue and then runs one fingertip along the top of my dress, dipping it into my cleavage.

"You're going to leave this on when I fuck you," he tells me. "That way I can pretend you're a Russian princess I kidnapped to ravage over and over again as many times as I want."

"Oh," I reply, relieved that at least I won't be naked as I prepare myself to pay up my part of our agreement.

"Lie down," he orders, taking a step back to reach down and undo the big skull king belt buckle on his jeans.

As I climb up on the bed, I try to remind myself of the previous times I've had sex and how quickly it's usually over. What's the longest any guy has been inside of me? Four or five minutes at most? All I have to do is lie down in my dress and a few thrusts later it will be done, and my parents will have two-hundred and fifty thousand dollars that can never be taken back.

I'm almost to the middle of the bed when his big hand wraps around my ankle and yanks me back toward the foot of the bed so hard that a yelp of surprise climbs up my throat.

"Wh-what are you doing?" I ask when I realize Miles is kneeling at the foot of his bed. He lifts my skirt and then his head disappears underneath it. His intention becomes obvious when his hot breath lands on the crotch of my panties before he reaches for the sides of the waistband and starts tugging them down my thighs.

"Shouldn't we...shouldn't we go slower? Get to know each other?" I ask.

His head pops up, carefully freeing my panties from my ankles, over my shoes that he doesn't seem to plan on removing.

"Right now, I want to get to know your pussy," Miles says before the blunt tip of one of his thick fingers I can't see slices through my lower lips, making me gasp. "But I can go slow with that."

Without giving me a chance to recover from his sensual touch, his head disappears back under the white lace of my dress, and then his hot, wet tongue leisurely follows the same path as his finger.

"Oh, my god!" I exclaim. The sensation causes my back to hit the mattress so hard I bounce. An unexpected rush of heat spreads through every inch of my body. The man hasn't even kissed my lips and now his mouth is...down there!

It's like a slow, gently rolling French kiss with his tongue delving a little deeper into my depths with each thrust. My back arches as I squirm, unable to figure out if I want to move away from his mouth or closer.

A wave of guilt and shame washes over me when I start enjoying what he's doing to me, but I quickly push it aside, reminding myself of the ring on my finger. I'm married to this man. I'm free to enjoy his tongue and the way it makes me feel even if I don't know him.

Yet, several long minutes later, my fists are both balled up in the comforter on either side of me and I'm still too tense to let go.

"You can, ah, stop. You don't have to..." I try to tell him as I stare up at his bedroom ceiling.

Miles bunches up the skirt of my dress until it's up to my hips, then raises his face to look at me. "I'm gonna lick your pussy until you come, princess," he says before his tongue goes back to work, making me moan and writhe when he flicks the tip of his tongue on my clit. God, it feels good. So good that I start to give into the wonderful sensation a little more.

"Faster," I whisper, because while slow is nice, he's finally hitting the perfect spot. "Ugh! Oh yeah, right there!" I shout when he complies, and my thighs start to shake. I've never, ever felt anything like this before, and I'm certain I'm about to reach the height of pleasure when I'm suddenly flipped to my stomach.

"What..." I start to ask when Miles slams every inch of his cock inside of me with one thrust, making my question turn into a scream.

"Holy fucking shit," he groans from above me as his chest lowers to my back, his much larger body pinning me underneath him.

His cock is big, so long and thick that it hurts at first as he pumps in and out of me while roughly gripping a fistful of the back of my hair. But then my body finally starts to relax and stretch to accommodate the invasion. My inner walls clench around his girth each time he enters me, trying to keep him deep inside me, enjoying that full feeling even though there's so much of him I can't even take a breath.

Miles' hips pump faster and faster as he grunts and curses above me with each one.

All it would take is the brush of my fingers on my clit and I would come, but when I try to reach underneath my body, Miles lets go of my hair and wrenches both of my arms behind my back, holding them down on my lower back.

"Not yet, princess. You'll come when I fucking say so and not before," he informs me before he pulls his cock completely free, making me whimper at the loss.

I don't get a chance to voice my complaint because Miles' tongue takes over, lapping at my clit again while he continues restraining my arms.

"Yesss," I gasp with my cheek pressed to the bed sheets. "Please don't...stop. Please Miles...please...Ugh!" I exclaim the last word in frustration when his mouth disappears yet again.

This time when he fills me, I'm a more active participant, slamming myself back onto his hard cock, chasing the release that's been so close three times now. I feel...out of control. Desperate.

"Touch me!" I plead with him.

Letting my arms go, Miles pulls me up by my hair until I'm on my knees, my back against his chest. His big tattooed left arm finally comes around and dives under my dress to cup me between my legs possessively. The sight of his dark, scary tattoos on the white lace looks wrong but oh so hot, touching me in such a naughty way. He still doesn't apply the pressure I need on my clit. I try to grind down on his palm but can't get the right angle which is so frustrating!

"You want to come?" Miles asks against my ear.

"Yes!" I sob.

His teeth nip roughly at my lobe while he continues to fill my pussy, dominating every inch of my entire body inside and out. I'm locked in his grip and couldn't move even if I wanted to.

"Not yet," he says, denying my pleasure and nearly making me weep because I'm so close.

"Please...it hurts," I tell him as the liquid warmth continues to build in my core. It feels like I'm going to burst if I don't get some relief and soon.

"I hurt too, princess," Miles growls, wrapping his other hand around my throat and then sliding it lower to jerk the top of my dress down. Freeing my breast, he palms it and gives it a squeeze that is almost painful, yet still nearly hurtles me over the edge of ecstasy. "My balls ache with the need to unload inside of your tight little cunt," he says.

"Do it," I moan while I reach down to cover his hand between my legs with my own to try and press it tighter against my flesh. "Do it...now!"

"Promise me, Kira," he says, and then he pulls his cock free, leaving the hard appendage pressing lewdly between the crease of my bottom while his bearded mouth sucks deeply on the side of my neck, no doubt leaving beard rash and hickeys.

"Anything," I say. I mean it, I would give the man anything he wants to make him move inside of me right this moment.

"Promise you won't leave me," he says between placing gentler kisses on my neck.

"I-I won't," I agree as some of the lust haze clears because of my confusion. I thought that was what I promised when I married him. In fact, I was expecting him to shoot for the stars and ask for a lifetime of blowjobs.

"I'm the only one who gets to fuck you now," Miles says as he lowers my upper body back down to the mattress, flattening me with his weight. He buries his cock inside me fully while his hand still squeezes my breast. "Say it!" he growls with a deeper shove inside of me.

"Only...only you," I whisper between gasps thanks to his palm starting to rub my pussy in such an amazing way that he has my eyes rolling back in my head.

"Oh fuck, here it comes!" he shouts. His cock swelling inside of me and his fingers circling my needy clit finally sends me over the edge.

"Yes! Yes! *Yessss!*" I scream as the pleasure explodes from every pore and my body trembles in wave after wave of ecstasy. My orgasm seems to go on and on forever, or maybe there are several thanks to the fingers still playing with my pussy, wringing every single drop of bliss from me.

When the shivers finally do stop and my head starts to clear, I realize Miles is still on top of my back, breathing heavy. Our sweaty bodies are pressed together with his cock lodged deep inside of me. His damp lips press kisses to my shoulder where my dress has come down while his hand between my legs seems content to keep stroking my pussy like it's his new favorite pet.

Sex has never felt *anything* like that before. Now I understand the concept of "mind-blowing" because I feel...different afterward, and my head is still fuzzy from the overload of sensations.

"Mmm-mmm," Miles groans, the deep vibrations echoing

through my back as he occasionally swivels his hips. "Incredible, princess."

"Mm," I agree.

"Hottest little pussy I've ever been in," he grunts. "You're dripping wet and burning me up so good I don't ever want to leave."

His comment should be a comforting thought, yet it has the opposite effect since it happens at the same time sticky liquid seeps out of me, coating my inner thighs, making an enormous damp spot on the comforter. God, it's embarrassing how wet I am for this man I don't even know.

A man that's now my husband.

Our marriage didn't seem real at the courthouse.

Or when I hugged my parents and told them goodbye.

But now it suddenly hits me that I've given myself to this stranger in every way. He paid for me and now I'm his.

Within a few minutes of great sex, he had me sobbing and begging, owning my body like it belonged to him and was no longer my own.

Miles finally removes his thick flesh from inside of me.

Why do I feel so empty now? He wasn't ever there before, and I was just fucking fine.

Most of his upper body weight is still on top of me when he lifts my skirt high enough that there's a breeze on my backside. Then his thick finger drags wickedly right down the crease of my ass down to my pussy which gives another needy spasm, causing more of my arousal to come gushing out of me.

"Goddamn," Miles grunts in that deep, husky smoker's voice while his finger keeps trailing up and down, up and down the most private part of me lewdly. "I wish you could see this cream pie we made. Mmm-mmm, that was fucking incredible. Can't wait to do it again. Maybe here..." I gasp when his fingertip presses against my puckered hole, touching me where no one else has ever touched me before. He pushes the tip of his finger inside, invading me and says, "It'll take a while, and hurt like hell at first as I squeeze in inch by inch, but eventually I'll make it all fit, just like I did in your tight little cunt. And you'll fucking love it. I bet you'll beg for more again..."

No, no, no.

This is all too much too soon from a man I don't know! And from the way he had me so strung out our first time, if I give in and sleep with him again, there's no telling what he could convince me to do, even things I've never *wanted* a man to do.

I was only supposed to marry him, not surrender my body to him to use however he wants. We were supposed to just have sex, the normal, quick kind that doesn't leave me feeling like a brainless ragdoll who is completely at his mercy. I may have given up my life for him, but I'm keeping my body and my dignity!

"I-I can't breathe," I say as I push myself up on shaking arms to try and escape.

CHAPTER TEN

Miles

ONE SECOND, I'm sweaty and spent, recovering from the best fuck of my life with the most gorgeous woman who also happens to be *my wife*. The next, she's scrambling out from underneath me, hiding her breasts with her arm across her body while trying to pull her dress up.

"Don't...don't touch me again," she says.

Confused doesn't even begin to describe what I'm feeling.

"We're married," I remind her. "I'm damn well going to touch my wife."

"I agreed to marry you and consummate the marriage. That's it!" she replies, turning her back to me.

"What's your problem?" I ask. "You loved every second and begged me to make you come!"

"I was faking it," she responds softly.

"Bullshit!" I exclaim.

"You...you made me beg by withholding."

"Then you came harder than you ever had before, didn't you?" I point out. "I need clean sheets because your pussy gushed all over them and my face."

I hear her gasp indignantly before she asks, "Where's the shower? I-I need a shower," and storms out of the room in search of the bathroom.

What the hell is her problem? The sex was too good? Is she expecting an apology for that?

"I'll go get your shit while you're acting insane!" I tell her retreating back.

Women.

How the fuck do men deal with the same one for long periods of time?

And holy shit.

It just occurred to me that while we were fucking, I made her promise not to leave me.

Kira probably thinks I'm the biggest pussy on the planet. Lord knows I feel like an insecure asshole.

Maybe she won't remember that part.

Hell, who am I kidding? I think I'll remember the details of our first time together until the day I die.

Based on how Kira responded to me, I'm guessing she will too.

Every. Single. Second.

Including me being a pussy.

Once I re-dress, I go down to her car and bring up all of her boxes, dropping them off in the living room. It takes me less than ten minutes. So, I grab a beer from the fridge and pace while sipping it, waiting for *my wife* to get out of the shower.

Ten more minutes pass, and then fifteen.

After an hour, I go over to turn the still locked bathroom door and then knock on it. "You alive in there?"

"Yes," is her one-word tearful response, making me feel like shit when I don't even know what I did wrong.

"I'm heading out. You want to come, or are you planning to hide in there all night?"

There's no response after a full minute, so I give up and leave, taking her car keys with me to Avalon.

"WHAT THE HELL are you doing here?" Coop asks when he climbs up on the stool beside mine at the bar when I'm on my third beer.

"What does it look like I'm doing?" I reply, tipping my bottle to him before I take a long swig.

I came to look at tits and ass, and there's plenty here right behind me.

But I'm not even looking at them, because doing so makes me feel like I was cheating thanks to the new weight on my ring finger.

How fucking stupid is that? My white gold wedding band looked like a plain piece of jewelry when Cooper first showed it to me before the ceremony. Now I'm pretty sure it's entirely responsible for tightening the invisible choke collar around my cock.

"You're drinking alone in a titty bar when you should be getting to know your new wife."

"I don't think she wants to know me," I tell him, the disappointment obvious in my sullen tone.

"Why do you say that?"

"Because she locked herself in the bathroom for over an hour. She was still in there when I left."

"Maybe she was sick or something was wrong. Did you check on her? Make sure she didn't bust her head and was lying on the floor bleeding out?" he asks.

"Oh, she was alive all right. I could hear her crying."

"Jesus! What the hell did you do to her?" he snaps at me.

"Nothing," I reply. "We fucked, and then she ran and hid."

"That...that's a bad sign," Coop says. "Did you hurt her...during?"

"I made her shake harder than an earthquake, but I didn't hurt her."

"She enjoyed herself? You're absolutely sure?"

"Yes! I'm absolutely fucking sure," I tell him. I can be a knucklehead, but I'm not that stupid. I've been with enough women to know when the sex is good for them too. Most of the time I honestly don't give a shit if they enjoy it since I'm just looking to get off. But with Kira, I wanted to make her feel good so she would want more.

And then, I blurted out that I wanted her to promise she wouldn't leave me like a nutless eunuch.

"When it was over, she said she couldn't breathe and then she freaked out," I explain to Cooper.

"You should go talk to her," he says. "Ask what's wrong. That's what husbands do."

"I'm not sure I'm cut out for all this," I say since I don't want to face her after the shit I said in the heat of the moment.

"Dude, it's only been a few hours! Why did you go through with the wedding if you weren't a hundred percent sure?"

"I dunno," I say before taking a swig from my beer. "It was stupid."

"Well, now it's done, so you need to figure this shit out, at least as long as Kira wants to stick around. It won't be long unless you find a way to not be a dick and make her happy."

"How the hell do I do that?" I ask him.

"No clue, but not leaving her by herself in a new house in a new city is probably a good start. She seems a little shy, and you are... brash. Give her some time to adjust to moving in and shit with you. Don't rush her or abandon her."

"So I should go home and stay there even if she hides in the bathroom all night?"

"She can't hide in there forever. Eventually she'll come out for something to eat or drink and you can feed her."

"I have to feed her?" I ask in confusion. "I thought wives were supposed to cook for their husbands. My mom always did."

"Welcome to the new age where wives are treated as equals. Most of them even have jobs outside the home, so the husband has to split the household chores equally."

"Oh," I mutter because I wasn't aware of all that. My whole life my mother just hopped from one rich dude to an even richer dude. Money was all she looked for in a husband, and in exchange she cooked for them and treated them like kings so they would keep her around. Now I guess that was because she really didn't want to have to find a job and take care of herself.

"You really should've talked to someone who is married before you went and did it," Cooper chuckles.

"I did. I heard Abe and Chase talking about how their old ladies wanted to fuck them all the time."

"They're trying to get pregnant! Most marriages are not sex all day, every day."

"Well, that's a shame," I say. "And I didn't expect Kira to be a sex slave, but I don't think she even likes me."

"She doesn't know you yet. Give her a chance to get to know you as well as I do. Then she can be certain she doesn't like you," he jokes.

"You're an asshole," I say even though he's right. She's not going to like me.

"Can't argue with that," Coop says with a grin.

"But the sex was fucking incredible. She'll definitely want it again, right?"

"No fucking idea, man. That's between you and her. But you can be a little..."

"What?" I ask.

"Intense. Take it down a few notches and talk to her."

"Yeah. Okay," I agree as I tip my beer back to finish it off so I can go face the music.

Kira

WHEN THE WATER goes cold in the bathtub again, I drain it and turn the faucet back on. The overhead light glints off of the ring on my finger, reminding me of the serious commitment I just made a few hours ago. It feels like I gave up a part of my soul in exchange for marrying him. A part that I won't ever get back.

I don't know how long I've been sitting in here; but judging by the wrinkles on my fingertips, it's been a while.

And I don't even know why I'm still hiding after Miles said he was leaving. I heard the door close and his bike start up outside, so I'm almost certain he's gone.

Despite however long I've been in the tub, his scent still clings to me like it's been permanently soaked up by the pores in my skin. I hate that he smells so good, spicy and masculine with hints of leather that I could become addicted to.

Eventually I even cave and grab his body wash to pour it into the running water so that the bubbles smell strongly of him. *My husband.*

I don't regret my decision to marry him to save my father's life and my parents' livelihood. I would do it all over again and maybe even more enthusiastically knowing what Miles looks like now and how good he is in bed.

So why am I sitting in his bathtub crying and looking like a prune?

I think it's all just a little overwhelming because I wasn't expecting to *enjoy* being with him. Who makes a deal with the devil and likes it? There has to be some sort of horrible catch that I haven't uncovered yet.

Honestly, I'm not sure if I've ever really enjoyed sex with any man. It was usually over before things started getting good for me.

Having a man so in control of my body was scary. Miles knew how to make me feel good, better than I know myself. Although, for a while there, it felt like he was torturing me. And while there was a little pain, there was a lot more pleasure. Sex with him felt good but wrong at the same time, as I lost all of my inhibitions. Miles made me feel drunk or high on some kind of drug I've never had before.

I've always been a good girl who doesn't want to let her parents down. I didn't try alcohol until the day I turned twenty-one. I've never smoked or used marijuana, much less any harder, illegal substances. And I didn't have sex until I was a senior in high school and eighteen, legally an adult making my own choices.

Despite the fact that I'm twenty-three, I'm not sure if I've ever really felt like an adult until today when I finally moved out of my parents' house, got married, and had really good sex with my new husband. Miles has obviously been with plenty of women. Now I'm incredibly embarrassed, because I have no clue what I'm doing in bed while he's on an expert level.

I don't know how to be on my own. And I definitely don't know how to be a wife. Sure, I've seen my mother and father together all these years, but Miles is nothing like my father, who is gentle and caring. Instead, Miles is tough, rugged and intimidating. He fucked me and never once kissed my lips. What kind of man does that? He didn't take my clothes off or his own. When I scrambled off the bed and finally got a good look at him, he was still wearing his t-shirt but not his leather cut, and he had simply shoved his jeans down to get inside of me without undressing.

I guess over the last few days I had been expecting a mild-mannered, dorky guy with tons of money instead of the rough-neck bad boy biker husband I got.

Which makes me wonder – how does he have so much money?

And why did he buy a wife?

CHAPTER ELEVEN

Miles

SINCE I HAVE no idea what Kira likes to eat, I decided to call in a pizza. Everyone likes pizza, right?

If she doesn't, I'll go find her something else.

For now, I better get home before the pizza delivery guy shows up so I can pay him.

Hopefully Kira's out of the bathroom by now and we can...talk.

What the hell are we supposed to talk about?

I have to admit that even if she doesn't say a word to me, I wouldn't mind just being in the same room with her, looking at her beautiful face and body. My cock twitches at just the reminder of being inside of her, fucking her while she was wearing her white, dainty wedding dress.

She may not have been a virgin, but I know for a fact she's never had anyone fuck her like I did. That much was obvious after she scurried off the bed and told me not to touch her again. And I won't, not unless she asks me to.

God, I hope she asks.

When I get to the house and unlock the door, I find her curled up on the sofa in a pair of pale green pajama pants and a matching tank top, sound asleep even after the noise I made coming in.

Or she's just pretending to be asleep so that I'll leave her alone.

Fine. Whatever.

Since I had planned on both of us sleeping in the bed, I don't have any extra blankets or anything else.

Peeling off the black comforter from the bed and grabbing one of the pillows, I take them into the living room to cover her up, even though doing so should be a sin because she's sexy as hell in pajamas. Then, I lift her head and carefully wedge the pillow between her and the sofa arm.

I go outside and smoke a joint while I wait for the pizza guy to make sure he doesn't knock and wake her up if she's really out.

By the time he arrives, I could eat the entire thing, but I don't, leaving three slices for Kira in case she wakes up hungry. There's not much in the house to eat, which means we'll have to take a trip to the grocery store tomorrow to stock up. It's not much of an outing, but at least it's something that will hopefully get the woman talking to me.

CHAPTER TWELVE

Kira

"Hey, mom," I say into the phone when she answers.

"Kira, how are you?" she asks, her voice concerned.

"I'm fine," I tell her.

"Did you...sleep well?" she asks.

"Yeah, I did," I reply, even though it's a lie. Then, there's a heavy silence between us because she would never ask if Miles and I slept together or were intimate, and I would never tell her that we were and that it was amazing, but then I crashed hard on the sofa.

When I woke up this morning with the sun shining through the windows, I was surprised that I slept all through the night and that Miles covered me up at some point with his bedding. I snuck past his room on the way to the shower and found him sleeping with just the thin, black sheet over part of his body, his thick chest and tattoos on full display.

Shaking those thoughts from my head, I ask my mother, "Did the money hit your account yesterday in time for Daddy to give it to Zeno?" I should've checked in with her yesterday, but there was a lot going on with the sex and sleeping like the dead. It must have been the catastrophic orgasm that put me out. I was planning to sleep in the bed with Miles; but since he covered me with the bedding, he must not have minded me sleeping alone.

"Yes," my mother thankfully answers. "We gave him the full amount owed."

"Good. That's good," I tell her, glad that mess is taken care of.

"Is he treating you well?" my mother blurts out.

"Yeah, he is," I assure her. "The house is small but nice, right near the ocean and the sound."

"That's good. Has he fed you? I can send you some stew!"

"Don't worry. I won't starve to death," I reply.

"When will we see you again?" she asks.

"I'm not sure. Soon," I say because I can't up and leave to go home right away. I'm not certain if Miles would let me even if I wanted to.

"What do you have planned for today?"

"No clue. Miles is in the shower." That's why I decided to call when I did, so that we could have a little more privacy.

"Oh. Well, hopefully you'll do something fun."

"Right, yeah," I agree just as Miles comes stomping into the living room fully dressed and sliding his sunglasses over his eyes. "I've got to go, but I'll talk to you soon," I say to my mother quickly.

"Love you, Kira."

"Love you too," I tell her before I end the call.

"We're leaving," Miles says.

"Where are we going?" I ask when I get to my feet, already dressed in my jeans and a dark blue tee after my early morning shower.

"Shopping," he replies which is the last place I imagined.

"Shopping for what?" I ask.

"House shit," he says. "Can we take your car?"

"Ah, yeah. Sure," I say since he still has the keys.

I follow Miles out to the deck where he locks the door. Then, once we're down the steps, he climbs into the driver seat of my car, which is fine with me. I don't know where anything is in this town.

Our first stop is at a furniture store, which of course makes me think of my parents and causes a pang of homesickness.

"Pick out whatever you want," Miles says when we walk inside. He flops down on the first sofa in sight without removing his sunglasses.

"Huh?" I ask in confusion.

"Whatever pictures or shit you want."

"I don't need anything," I tell him. "It's your house, so you should put whatever you want in it."

"It's your house now too," he grumbles.

"Are you gonna help?" I ask.

"Nope."

"What if you hate what I pick out?"

"I won't."

"Okay," I say with a sigh before I start making a lap around the store.

I'm trying to decide between two beach paintings when a short, older man with a white beard comes up beside me and asks, "Anything I can help you with today?"

"Oh, hi. I was just trying to decide between these pictures."

"Both are lovely," he says. "And by the same local artist."

"They're beautiful," I say. "But I'm not sure which I like more, the lighthouse or the wild horse grazing."

"We'll take both."

The two of us turn around in surprise when Miles suddenly speaks up from behind us.

"Of course," the old man says, immediately taking two steps away from me. "Is there anything else I can do for you today, sir?"

"We don't have to get both," I tell Miles.

"You like them both?" he asks.

"Yes, but..."

"Then we're getting both."

"I'll go wrap them and ring them up at the register," the old man says before quickly removing them from the wall and scurrying away.

"Are you sure?" I ask Miles in concern. "They're like a thousand dollars each and you have to look at them too."

"They're both fine. I repaired a shit ton of steps in that light-house, and I've seen the horses on Shackleford Banks a few times."

"Oh," I reply in surprise. Before I can ask him if he's lived here long, he stomps over to the register like I've somehow pissed him off.

A few minutes later, we're back in the car, but he doesn't take the road back to his house.

"We need food," he grumbles.

"Okay."

"What do you like to eat?" he asks.

"Anything is fine."

"That's not an answer," he huffs, like I'm a big pain in his ass.

"I'm not picky."

"Obviously not if you agreed to marry me."

I could've done worse, I think to myself. Miles is nothing like the worst-case scenario I imagined all week. He's not old and wrinkly. And I can't figure out if he's grumpy all the time or just to me because of last night when I flipped out. Or maybe I've done something else wrong. Either way, he doesn't seem very happy with me.

CHAPTER THIRTEEN

Miles

"WHAT DO YOU EAT FOR BREAKFAST?" I ask Kira as we stroll through the supercenter.

I'm pushing a fucking shopping cart, which is a first, but I figured I couldn't carry a week's worth of food in my arms.

And Kira? Well, her arms are wrapped protectively around herself and she's sticking to a two feet minimum distance behind me. Still, despite her discomfort, I have to say I love being out in public with her so everyone can see the ring on her finger. She belongs to me even though it feels like a million miles exist between us.

"Anything is fine," she says again, sounding like a broken record because it's been her response to every question I've asked her. This is quickly becoming infuriating. Especially since Cooper said I'm supposed to be talking to her and getting to know her. I'm making a goddamn effort here, and she won't even give me a hint of what kind of food she likes.

Stopping the cart in the middle of the cereal aisle, I turn around to face her. "Anything is not fine! You have to have likes or dislikes, so just tell me *something*, for fuck's sake!"

She cringes away from me when I raise my voice, causing the two old women in the aisle to glare at me like I'm an abusive husband.

And it may very well come to that, because I'm certain pulling her teeth out one by one would literally be easier than getting her to open up.

Rather than give me a verbal response, she walks over and grabs a box of Cheerios and places it in the cart.

"Was that so hard?" I ask with a huff. "We're not leaving until you fill this damn thing up with shit to eat. Got it, princess?"

"Yes," she responds.

And that's the last word she says before we get to the checkout counter. At least she did like I asked and added more items. Kira apparently also likes strawberry Poptarts, frozen waffles, bacon, lettuce and tomatoes I'm guessing for sandwiches, and BBQ potato chips.

"So based on your odd food selections, I take it you don't cook?" I ask Kira as we walk back to her car in the parking lot.

When she doesn't bother to give me a verbal response, I glance over my shoulder to see if she's maybe nodding or some shit.

But she's not there.

"Shit!" I exclaim as I abandon the cart to jog back up to the front of the store, my heart attempting to thump its way out of my chest as I try to figure out if she disappeared to go back home or if someone grabbed her. Since I have the keys to her car, it doesn't make sense that she would try to run.

I'm about to go through the sliding doors again to ask for security footage when I do a double take at the kids standing over to the right. I finally recognize her straight, brown hair trailing down her back between two kids and blow out a puff of air in relief.

Kira's kneeling down with her back to me, so I walk over to see what the hell was so damn important she ran off without telling me.

But then I see the smile on her face, and my anger disappears.

It's the only time I've seen her looking so...bright and happy. It doesn't take long to see the cause either. There's a black puppy squirming in her hands.

So I cross my arms over my chest and wait.

"Look how cute," Kira says when she straightens and holds the puppy out for me to see it.

"Yeah, cute," I mutter.

Her eyes finally face me head on, and she asks, "Where are the groceries?"

"Back at the car. Would've been nice if you had mentioned you were making a pit stop."

"Sorry," she replies softly, her face falling before she crouches down to put the mutt back into the cardboard box. Which is a shame because the woman was so stunning when she smiled that it felt like the world stopped spinning.

No. Hell no. I'm not really thinking of giving in on this, am I? I hate animals, especially dogs. They never like me and start barking non-stop when I'm around, as if they can smell the killer in me.

Even Eddie's dog Sparky, who I've been around for years, still growls and snaps his teeth at me if I get too close to him, and he wouldn't hurt a fly.

"Pick the dog back up," I tell her.

"What?" she asks.

"Pick it up," I repeat slowly.

Kira hesitates but eventually listens to me. And when she lifts the squirming mutt in the air again, it's like watching magic. A switch is flipped, and she's all beaming sunshine or whatever again.

"You can hold it in the car while I go back and get the food and shit he'll need."

"Seriously?" Kira asks, hitting me with her mega-watt smile.

"Seriously," I agree. "What do we owe you?" I ask the teenager who's responsible for causing me to make this insane decision.

"Nothing," he replies. "We just want them to go to good homes." He eyes me suspiciously like he's not certain I fit the bill.

"She'll take good care of him," I assure him, while pulling a twenty from my pocket and handing it over. It's the least I can do for making Kira happy.

"Thanks, man," he replies with a grin when he takes the bill.

"Come on," I tell Kira. "Let's see if anyone's stolen our groceries yet."

"Sorry," she tells me yet again.

"Save the apologies for when that little bastard chews up all my shit," I grumble.

After the groceries are loaded up in the trunk of the car, I open the passenger door for Kira to sit down with the dog.

"I'll grab his food and be right back," I tell her, even though I don't like leaving her here alone in the parking lot.

"Okay, thanks," she says. "Don't forget a bowl. He may need some flea medicine too. Oh, and a chew toy!"

Her excitement is cute. So cute that I say, "Do you want to come back in too?"

"Yes, but dogs aren't allowed," she points out.

"Hand him over," I say.

"What? Why?" Kira asks, clutching him to her chest as if she's afraid I'm going to hurt him. I may be a murderer, but I'm not a monster that goes around hurting innocent animals.

"I'll hide him so we can both go back," I explain. Even if an employee sees me with him, it's not like they would say a word. The Savage Kings have a reputation in town, one that people respect even if they don't approve.

Finally, Kira holds the mutt up to me, so I take him in one hand and unzip the inside pocket on my cut with my other. A little more than half his body fits since it was made to hold a big gun. And after I button up the front of my cut most of the way, you can't see his big round head sticking out.

"That actually works," Kira agrees with a puff of laughter that even makes my lips twitch.

"You're pushing the cart this time," I tell her.

"Sure," she replies happily, grabbing the one we just unloaded. "I really hope he doesn't pee on you."

"That makes two of us," I grumble before we march back into the store to stock up on dog supplies.

CHAPTER FOURTEEN

Kira

"My parents never let me have any pets," I tell Miles when we put our new puppy down in his backyard and watch him bounce around. I think we bought every dog item in the store for him, even a playpen for him to sleep in at night or if we leave, so he should be all set.

"Why not?" Miles asks.

"Because we were never home. And they didn't want dogs or cats at the store."

"What kind of store do they have?"

"Furniture. My dad makes everything by hand."

"Nice," Miles replies, his arms crossed over his leather vest, dark aviator sunglasses hiding his eyes. When I first saw him in the chapel, I thought the leather biker thing was intimidating, but that was before I watched him stuff a puppy into it. "What are you gonna name him?" he asks.

"How about...Blackjack and call him Jack for short?"

"That's a good name," he agrees with a hint of a smile on his sensual lips. Lips that have been on very intimate places of my body.

Miles has seen me come completely undone. Heck, he was the person who made me that way. In contrast, he's always so cool, calm and in control, never appearing to doubt himself for even a second.

And now I'm a nervous wreck around him, especially after seeing this softer side – the one that let me bring home a puppy to make me happy, even though he clearly doesn't care for them.

Do all women melt into desperate, begging puddles when they're in bed with him, or was that just me?

I need to get my head out of the gutter, which is why I ask, "So what do you do?"

"What do I do?" Miles repeats.

"To earn a living? Pay for things?"

Uncrossing his arms, he gives the opening of his leather vest a tug. "I'm a Savage King."

"What's that?"

"A brotherhood of men who ride Harleys," he replies.

"But how does riding Harleys amass the type of wealth you have?"

"We own most of the major businesses in town and each get a cut of the proceeds for keeping the city safe."

"Oh," I mutter. "So you're like a civilian law enforcement group?"

"Something like that," he answers.

"Is it okay if I get a job?" I ask.

"Why the hell do you want a job when you have half a million dollars?"

Shrugging my shoulders, I say, "To have something to do."

"You have something to do now – take care of the mutt. Anything you need, I'll buy."

"So, are you telling me I can't get a job?"

"No," he says with a heavy exhale. "I'm just saying you don't need to."

"And I can leave whenever I want?"

"You're not a prisoner," he mutters.

"Then can I have my car keys back?"

Miles stares at me through his dark shades for several silent seconds before he pulls my keyring from his pocket and tosses them to me.

"I would like to know where you're going when you leave and when you'll be back," he says. "At least leave a note or something so that I won't worry –." His words cut off abruptly like he was about to say more but changed his mind.

"Will you do the same?" I ask since I didn't know where he went last night or when he was coming back.

"Yeah," he responds while scratching the scruff on the side of his face. "Yeah, I can do that."

"Okay. Thanks."

Miles

KIRA WANTS to know where I'm going?

I guess that's a typical wife thing, even though I haven't been accountable to anyone since I was thirteen.

Does that mean she doesn't want me around or she does?

Fuck, it's hard to get anything out of this woman. And I can't come right out and ask like a pussy. Me and vulnerability don't mix at all.

At least she seems to like having the dog. There haven't been any more tears today, so that's a plus. While I'm standing there staring at her, trying to figure out what to say next, I hear a low grumble reverberate through the air.

"Was that you or the dog?" I ask, trying to conceal a smile.

"It was me," Kira says sheepishly. "I don't really feel hungry, but I guess my stomach is pretty empty."

"Well, I'm hungry," I tell her. "You want me to make you something? I was thinking about scrambling some eggs and making some bacon."

"Breakfast for dinner? That would be great," Kira replies, flashing me that dazzling smile again as the puppy tumbles over to her feet. "I'll come in and help you in just a second."

I give her a nod, but her attention is already back on the dog. I head back inside, digging into the refrigerator to get the eggs and bacon out, then cracking open a can of beer.

"Beer and eggs? Yuck!" Kira comments when she comes back inside and sees what I'm doing.

"Cooking is hot work out here on the coast, have to stay hydrated," I tell her in mock seriousness. She pulls a bottle of water out of the refrigerator and the gallon of milk, then stands beside me at the counter.

"You add anything to those eggs yet?" she asks, nodding to the bowl I'm whisking with a fork.

"They're eggs," I reply. "Always thought they were a stand-alone dish."

"Oh boy, let me hold that," she says as she reaches over and takes the bowl from me. "You go work on the bacon. That's a manly job."

"Not really," I snort, picking up the paper plate where I had spread the meat on a paper towel, and heading over to the microwave.

"Wait!" Kira stop me. "I know you're not going to stick that in the microwave. You are an absolute terror in the kitchen. Set that down by the oven and heat up the pan for me, I'll cook the bacon first and then scramble the eggs with a little bit of the grease."

"You going to pour milk into them?" I ask skeptically.

"Uh, yeah," Kira rolls her eyes. "It's how you get them fluffy!"

"Fluffy!" I snort as I put the bacon down and grab my beer.

"Okay then. I'm going to turn on the TV. Call me if you need any help."

"I see, too manly for fluffy eggs, eh? Don't worry, I'll handle it this time, but in the future, I want you to cook with me. Who knows, it could be a good bonding experience."

I give her another snort and then grab the remote, flipping on the television. It only takes me a moment to realize that the episode of "River Monsters" is one I've already seen; and after absorbing Kira's words about a bonding experience, I decide to give it a shot. I leave the show on behind me as I turn back to the kitchen.

"Show me," I say as I walk up and lay a hand on her hip. She startles a little bit and tenses up, so I drop my hand and move to the counter beside her. "Sorry," I mutter.

"No worries, you just surprised me," Kira says with a blush rising in her cheeks. "I guess I got a little bit too invested in frying up perfect bacon. This will be the first thing I ever cook for you, and I guess I want it to be…"

"Perfect." I finish the sentence for her.

"Yeah," Kira agrees, giving me a brief smile. "I want it to be good, for both of us. I'm going to try."

"I'm going to do the same," I reply, reaching over to brush her hair back over her shoulder, being careful not to touch her skin. "I might be set in some of my rough and not-so-fluffy ways, but I promise you, I will try."

CHAPTER FIFTEEN

Kira

WE'VE ONLY LIVED TOGETHER for a few days, but I'm already starting to get to know more about the stranger I married.

He eats a lot of bacon, drinks gallons of beer, stays out late often, and never takes off his wedding ring. Not that I take mine off either. It's just comforting to see the piece of jewelry on his tough, masculine, tattooed hand even though we barely talk, making me feel like we're still in this together. But the most peculiar thing about Miles is he watches a lot of *Animal Planet*.

My dad loved to watch sports, usually soccer or hockey, so that's what I grew up having to endure. Even though I love animals, I find his choice of entertainment a bit odd.

I thought for sure a tough guy like Miles would prefer to sit back and enjoy fights, race cars, or something else masculine on television.

Instead, he watches wild animals and nature shows.

Unable to hold my tongue any longer, I finally breakdown and ask him one afternoon.

"Why *Animal Planet?*"

"Huh?" Miles replies while glancing over at me on the opposite end of the sofa.

"You watch this channel a lot. Is there a reason?"

"I don't know. I guess I envy the animals," he says before taking a swig of his beer, then resting the bottom on the top of his jean-covered thigh again.

"Why do you envy them?" I ask since he seems to be doing pretty well for himself.

"Their lives are simple," he explains when his gaze returns to the flat screen. "They eat, sleep, fight, fuck and kill whenever the hell they want without any judgment. Humans need reasons and explanations for every damn thing. It's exhausting."

"Oh," I say as if I understand what he's talking about.

"Besides, they have a lot of those wildlife cop shows. I thought about being a cop when I was younger."

Miles' expression darkens, and he quickly finishes off the rest of his beer. I can tell there's a story there, so I ask him, "It seems like you ended up a long way from that life. Did something happen to change your mind or set you on a different path?"

"Yeah," Miles grunts. Without any further explanation, he gets up to throw away his can and get another beer.

"You got any big plans for tomorrow?" Miles asks me when he returns, clearly trying to steer the subject to something else. I don't want to push him on his past until he is ready, so I let it pass for now.

"I was actually thinking about going over to the animal shelter tomorrow and volunteering for a few hours."

"Volunteering to do what?" Miles asks as he cracks open the can. I notice he can do it with only one hand, and I can't help but be slightly impressed.

"You know, clean out cages, feed animals, play with them and make sure they're not getting lonely."

"Have fun with that," Miles snorts.

"Well, I was thinking, if you're not busy..." I trail off expectantly.

"What, you want me to come? To clean up dog shit? I would rather..." Miles begins, but then after looking at me for a moment, his expression softens and he sighs. "If you want, yeah, I'll come with you. But you're dealing with the shit!"

"Deal," I grin. "It will be fun, you'll see. A lot of the animals there have been abandoned and are desperate for attention. They'll love you!"

"Well...we'll see," Miles sighs. "I have to warn you; the way Blackjack has acted towards me isn't usual. The dogs probably won't think much of me."

"Blackjack adores you. What are you talking about?" I protest. I reach down to rub the puppy, who is sleeping at my feet; then pick him up to hold him out to Miles. As soon as he gets close, Blackjack begins licking the air frantically, trying to get close enough for a kiss.

Miles reaches over to take him from me and lets the puppy squirm all over him before setting him back down on the floor. "That little skunk would love anyone who fed him, that's all. I'm going to head to bed. Just let me know when you're ready to go tomorrow. You going to hang out in here?"

"Yeah, I guess I'll stay up a while," I reply, uncertain of Miles' intentions. Does he want me to come to bed with him? Does he just want to sleep, or something more? I wish he wasn't so damned hard to read!

Before I can think of anything else to say or do, Miles mutters, "Good night," and walks away. *We seemed to be getting along so well for a moment there,* I think as I wrap myself in my blanket on the couch. How does it always switch back to being so awkward so quickly?

THE NEXT MORNING Blackjack wakes me up early whining to go for a walk. By the time we return, I can already hear the shower running, so I know Miles is awake. I start the coffee and then gather my clothes together so I can take over the bathroom once he's done.

"Good morning," he nods to me as we pass each other in the hallway. "I'll be ready when you are."

"Okay," I say to his back as he walks away. "I made coffee!" I call down the hall, then duck into the steamy bathroom. God, the man takes thousand-degree showers. The air in the bathroom is absolutely stifling.

I get ready quickly, not bothering with much make-up since we're not going to be doing anything too glamorous today. When I emerge from the bathroom in my tank top and cut-off shorts, Miles just stares at me from the couch.

"Everything okay?" I ask him, suddenly concerned that I'm dressed too far down, and trying to remember if he's seen me without makeup so far.

"Yeah, yeah, we're good," Miles replies with a shake of his head. "You okay with taking my bike?"

"Sure, that will be fun," I reply, trying to hide the nervous tremor in my voice. I've been thinking some inappropriate thoughts about riding on his motorcycle and have only recently realized just how intimate a process it actually can be.

Once we're outside, Miles hands me a helmet, then climbs onto his motorcycle and starts it while I fumble with the straps under my chin. Watching me with the hint of a smile across his full lips, he finally motions me closer and deftly fastens the helmet for me. I take a moment to look at his long, muscular frame holding the Harley up straight before I throw a leg over the seat behind him, then try to situate my feet on the pegs.

"Lean forward into me," Miles calls back to me before he starts moving.

I press my chest against the back of his leather cut, feeling the raised edges of his patch press into my breasts. I tentatively lay my hands on the sides of his hips. "You're going to want to hold on tight," he says with a hint of laughter in his voice, before twisting the throttle and dropping the bike into gear.

I squeeze my eyes shut as the wind tears at my eyes, gasping as the air is ripped from my lungs. I feel Miles shift and realize that I've practically got him in the Heimlich maneuver, my fists knotted together and pressed into his belly so hard it's amazing he can even breathe. "Are you laughing?" I yell as I feel his shoulders rising and falling unsteadily.

"I'm trying not to, I swear!" he yells back over the roar of the engine. "I've never had anyone tickle me so badly while riding!"

"You're ticklish?" I cry in delight, poking a finger into his side.

The sudden swerve of the bike forces my hand back around the front of Miles' cut, and the sounds of our laughter mixing trail after us as we continue our ride. In only a few minutes, and without any further reckless tickles, we arrive at the county animal shelter.

"I bet you won't do that again," Miles says as he kills the engine and leans the bike over on its kickstand.

"Not while we're on the motorcycle, but I might try and ambush you with a tickle now and then. You'll just have to wait and see, won't you?"

"You seemed to be having fun at least," Miles observes as we walk into the shelter together.

"I think I did," I reply. "It's a good thing too, because it looks like we might be doing that a lot together."

"Yeah, if you hang around with me long enough, you might even learn to ride yourself."

"Who said I can't?" I tease him.

The shelter had just opened, so when the two of us appear at the front desk and let them know we would like to volunteer to help clean, the staff are more than happy for the assistance. After showing us where to find the cleaning supplies, and having us sign some waivers, the two of us are escorted into a long room full of cages, filled with the sounds of barking, howling animals.

"God, this is hell," Miles mutters. He has a bag of dog food thrown over his shoulder, which he sits down and then slashes open with a knife he draws from his belt. "I'm going to try and feed this first guy but be ready for the worst."

As soon as Miles approaches the cage, the dog, a small, scruffy looking mutt, charges the gate growling and snarling. Miles jumps back, then turns to me sheepishly. "Maybe you should just pass me the bowl," he mutters.

"That might be best," I grin as I stroll past him, the small dog immediately sitting down with its tail wagging joyfully. I open the cage and reach in to rub his short, coarse fur, then grab the empty bowl and pass it out to Miles. A moment later, I place the full bowl back inside the cage and give the dog another quick rub on his back as he digs in, his entire rear end wagging furiously.

"I don't know why they act that way towards me," Miles says with a hint of sadness.

"You're intimidating," I tell him with a shrug. "I kind of felt the same way when I first saw you. Just a little scared..."

"Don't say that," Miles interrupts me sharply. Softening his tone, he continues, "That's never what I intended, not for you. I don't want to scare you."

"You don't now. Not quite as much," I tell him with a grin.

We move through the rows of cages, Miles staying well back as we continue feeding and watering the animals as needed, the two of us finishing the area in just under an hour. "Okay," I tell Miles, "Now we're on to the cats!"

Miles groans audibly, but otherwise follows along dutifully as we walk to the side of the building where the cat cages are kept. An older woman is already in there, scooping out cat litter from a cage low to the floor.

"Oh, hello there, you two," she says as she pets the cat inside the cage before closing the door. "I've almost finished up in here, except for that top row there. My old shoulders aren't too good at overhead work anymore, and honestly, that orange fellow on the end there is a vicious sort."

"Oh, the poor thing," I croon as I approach the cage, peering in to try and see if the cat appeared obviously abused. When an orange paw filled with bared razors lashes out through the grate, I quickly jerk back.

"Damn," Miles mutters as the cat presses his face to the cage door to hiss at me. "Might want to pass on that one. He's one angry little dude."

"Wait, Miles, keep talking," I tell him when the cat suddenly stops hissing, its ears perking up to listen to Miles' voice.

"What? You want me to talk to the cat?" Miles says as he points to the cage. "Hey, he does seem to be calming down," he observes as he moves closer. "Here, kitty, kitty, kitty," he calls. "You're a good little puss-puss. Please don't claw my eyes out, kitty-kitty."

As he approaches the gate, the orange cat visibly relaxes, folding its front paws under its chest as it laid down near the gate, then rubbing the side of its face against the cage door as Miles draws close. "Well, look at that," Miles says in wonder. "If I didn't know any better, I'd think the clever little bastard was trying to lure me close so he could eat me."

"Do you want to try to open the cage and see if he'll let you touch him?" I ask. "I'm not saying you should," I quickly add.

"No, no, let's play this out," Miles says as he lifts the latch on the cage. "I've never tried to deal much with cats. This is kind of...I don't know, if he actually likes me, it's kind of cool." As Miles opens the gate, the cat stands up; but instead of hissing or clawing at him, it lets out a long, plaintive 'meow', then stretches its neck out to sniff at Miles' face.

"Hey, buddy," Miles croons as he reaches up to scratch the cat's side. When it becomes clear that the animal will allow it, Miles scoops the cat up and cradles it to his chest, turning back to me with a huge grin on his face.

"That cat looks like it's smiling as much as you are," I observe as he continues rubbing the bright orange fur. "Here, I'll clean up his cage while you two entertain each other."

LANE HART & D.B. WEST

"I can't believe he actually likes me," Miles says as I works on the cage. "I've never seen any animal react like this to me."

"Maybe he knew he couldn't intimidate you," I joke with him. "Or maybe just the sight of you struck such fear into him he knew he had to change his tune!"

"That's not it, is it, kitty-kitty?" Miles purrs. "Who's a sweet boy? You're a sweet boy!" he continues, now cradling the vicious orange devil like a baby.

Once I get done with the cage, Miles reluctantly puts the cat back in, patting him one more time before he sets the latch. The cat lets out one more long, sad 'meow' before Miles turns away. As I study his face, for a brief moment, I see something in his eyes that causes a stab of pain in my heart.

"You all right?" I ask Miles gently.

"I think he really liked me," Miles shrugs.

"Is that so unbelievable? That someone could like you that much?"

"I don't know," Miles replies, his voice hardening and the brief moment of sadness passing. "I'm just not used to it, that's all. Come on, we all done here?" he asks gruffly.

This time I see right through his tough guy façade and know that if he spent much more time here, he would end up running a cat rescue out of his house. *Our* house. "Yeah, that's all for today. Let's get out of here, go get some lunch."

"Hey," Miles stops me with a light touch on my arm before we left the room. "Thanks for bringing me here. I mean, it was nasty as hell, but...thanks. I think I needed something like this."

"We can do it again, you and me," I reassure him. "Keep an open mind, there's no telling what sort of wild things we'll show each other."

CHAPTER SIXTEEN

Kira

IT'S A BEAUTIFUL DAY, not too chilly. So, after I take Jack out, I decide to walk down to the beach.

Of course I leave a note for Miles; because for the past few weeks, he's been leaving me notes telling me whenever he goes to the Savage Asylum, whatever that is. He's never invited me, and I've never asked, trying to avoid becoming a nagging wife.

When I get through the public access path, there's a volleyball net to the right with a group of people playing on either side.

They're all laughing and joking. It looks like they're having fun.

I take a seat in the sand to watch the waves roll in, soaking up the sun and the salty scent that reminds me of home.

This is the first time I've been away for more than a week, and I miss my parents.

Each morning I call and talk to them to check in, which makes me sad for the rest of the day when Miles leaves me home alone with Jack.

I want more here in my new home. I've never felt so lonely living with someone else. Miles barely talks unless it's to ask what I want to eat. He gets takeout from so many amazing restaurants that I've probably gained ten pounds since I got here.

I've been eating my feelings, which also makes me sad.

Why can't Miles just open up and talk to me about what he does every day, or offer to take me with him when he leaves the house? The day we went to the animal shelter together was great, but I've been going back on my own ever since because he declines my offer to join me. Which is confusing because I thought he had a good time. Guess I was wrong.

Is this how the rest of my life is going to be? Boring while I sit alone at home with the dog?

I could take Jack and go visit my parents for a few days, but I'm afraid that Miles will get angry because I want to leave, especially after our wedding night when he made me promise not to leave him.

So I won't just yet.

Maybe in a few weeks he'll trust me that, when I leave for a few days, I will come back.

When the white volleyball comes rolling up beside me, I snap out of my inner musings to stand up and serve it back to the group.

"Thanks!" the blonde girl that catches it says. Then she starts over to me instead of back to the waiting group at the net. "You play?" she asks.

"Ah, I played a little, in high school."

"We're a player short on our side if you want to join us?" she offers.

"Oh, yeah. If you're sure?" I ask since I don't want to intrude on their game.

"Come on," she says with a tilt of her head toward the net. "I'm Kelly, by the way. I'll introduce you to the rest of the guys."

"I'm Kira," I tell her.

"Well, Kira," she says when she tosses me the ball. "You're serving for us this time, and we're gonna kick some ass."

Miles

I'M NOT all that surprised when I come home from the Savage Asylum and Kira's not there.

"Where did she go today?" I ask Blackjack after I crouch down and give the hyper little shit a rub behind his ears.

Hell, I would love to go wherever my wife goes all day, every day, but I can't take the torture of wanting to not only touch her but strip her naked and fuck her on the nearest hard surface. I've been trying to keep those urges in check since the feeling is apparently not mutual if she still refuses to sleep in the same bed with me. And I'm trying my damnedest to figure out how to talk to her without pouring out my guts like a pussy and epically failing.

If Kira gets to know the real me, she'll bolt. Of that, I'm certain.

When I stand back up from spoiling the mutt, I see a note on the kitchen counter in her usual spot.

"*Gone to the beach,*" it says.

She doesn't say when she left.

For all I know she could've been gone for hours because someone kidnapped her, or she drowned...

Nah, the water is still too cold for swimming.

What if Kira didn't know that and tried to go, then her arms and legs froze so she couldn't swim back to shore?

Now I'm just being ridiculous. The obsession of my protectiveness of her knows no bounds.

Since Blackjack isn't barking to tell me he needs to go outside for a piss, she probably hasn't been gone long.

There's just one main public beach access close to the house, so that's where I head out to on foot.

It doesn't take long for me to spot my beautiful wife wearing a white t-shirt with some logo on it and black yoga pants that only come down to her knees. She's playing volleyball with a group of guys and girls who look her age – like they're on a break from college classes and hanging out at the beach on a nice, sunny day.

Kira looks happy, smiling in a way she only does for Blackjack or the dogs and cats at the animal shelter.

Fuck, she's gorgeous and sexy as hell. Whenever she jumps for the ball, her small perky tits bounce, making me yearn to feel them and taste them again.

And I'm jealous.

Jealous because these jackasses have been playing with her, seeing her sweet tits jiggling, and there's nothing I can do about it.

I can't go grab her up, throw her over my shoulder and show them who she belongs to. Kira doesn't want me to touch her.

She barely even looks at me when we're in the same room together.

It's become obvious that she doesn't want me or want to be married to me. She's just a sweet girl who is going to endure a year with me for the money, and then I'll never see her again.

And there's not a goddamn thing I can do to stop her.

Kira

"Do you know that hot Savage King who's watching you like a hawk?" Kelly asks. "I'm not sure if he's pissed or thinking about fucking you."

"Um, yeah, that's, ah, my husband," I respond.

"You're married to a King? Holy shit," she says in awe. "Those guys are dangerous and damn fine."

"They are," I agree as I glance over at Miles, who is glowering at us from the sand dunes. His arms are crossed over his wide, muscular chest, and aviator sunglasses cover his eyes like usual. I think his arms only uncross when he's eating or riding his motorcycle.

"I better go," I tell Kelly.

"Good luck," she says. I wave goodbye to the other players and then trudge through the sand to where my husband is waiting.

"Are you mad at me?" I ask him. "I left a note."

"I'm not mad," he grumbles before turning and walking away.

"Oh," I say in surprise as I follow him through the dunes back to the street that leads to his house. Does that mean Kelly was right? If he's not angry, he wants to...be with me again?

When we walk through the front door though, Miles heads to the bathroom and turns on the shower. I take Blackjack outside for a walk, more confused than ever.

It seems like the man is either hot or cold, nothing in between.

He's never kissed my lips, but he has kissed...other places on my body.

He keeps distance between us at all times, in the kitchen, in the hallway, on the sofa, as if he's trying to avoid any incidental physical contact.

I sleep on the sofa, and he doesn't seem to care since he's never asked me to come to bed with him.

If he wanted me, he would ask me to sleep with him, wouldn't he?

God, it feels like I need some type of tough guy decoder to figure out what he wants.

CHAPTER SEVENTEEN

Miles

"How's it going, man?" Frank, my barber, asks when I sit down in his chair.

"Been better," I mutter as the understatement of the century. For four weeks I've been carrying around the worst case of blue balls ever.

My wife is hot.

And I can't touch her. The most fucked-up thing is that I've never been the monogamous type, yet the thought of getting a club girl on her knees to give me relief, cheating on Kira in any way shape or form is blasphemy. Just thinking about it while we're married makes me feel shitty, so that's out too.

I'm fucking stuck.

"Lady problems?" Frank guesses.

"How'd you know?" I ask.

"Nothing with the club seems to ever get you down. Only other thing it could be is a woman."

"Yeah, yeah it is," I agree. Since I can't talk about this to anyone else but Cooper, I tell him, "I got married actually."

"Married?" Frank says when he comes to stand in front of me, his hand holding the electric razor frozen in the air. "No shit?"

"No shit," I grumble. "And she won't let me touch her. I don't think she even likes me. This isn't going to fucking work," I admit aloud the thoughts that have been racking my brain for almost a month.

"Women are...fickle," Frank tells me when he goes back to work shaving the side of my head. "I've been married for almost twenty years, and I still don't know what's going on in my woman's head. Sometimes she gets pissed at me for no reason. And when I ask what I did wrong, she says, *'Oh, you know exactly what you did!'* when I honestly have no fucking idea."

"That sucks, man," I tell him with a chuckle.

"I couldn't even tell you how long it's been since I got laid. A different president was probably in office."

"How the hell do you deal with that?" I ask him. "You get some on the side?"

"Fuck, no. Margie would cut off my balls if I wandered."

"So, you just suck it up and suffer? That's all you can do?" I grumble in disbelief.

Lowering the razor from my head to meet my eyes in the mirror, he says, "Do you love her?"

"What?" I ask.

"If you love her, then it's worth not getting laid. And you will get some. Eventually," he says with a grin. "When it happens, it's all worth it. I can't imagine my life without my Margie."

"Things are different for us," I tell him, withholding from him the fact that my cold, dead heart is not capable of ever loving someone. "She couldn't ever love an asshole like me. There's no way she's going to want to stick around."

"That's the beauty of it! The right woman can overlook all of your flaws. Maybe this girl is it, maybe not. But when you do find her? You better not let her go."

Kira

IT'S BEEN ALMOST a month since I married Miles, and he hasn't taken me again or even put his hands on me once.

I can't figure out if I'm happy about that or disappointed.

Oh, screw it, I'm definitely disappointed.

Was our first time not good for him? He wasn't the one screaming, sobbing, or begging. Nope, that was all me. So I'm guessing he didn't enjoy himself enough to ask me to join him in his bed.

That's right, I've been sleeping on the leather sofa for weeks! It's actually pretty comfortable. Just not as comfortable as a bed, and it lacks other additional benefits.

Several times I've been soaking in a warm tub filled with bubbles and found my hand disappearing between my legs to stop the throbbing ache.

I've never ached for sex before. In fact, I went years without it, including self-love.

The coastal weather has turned warm even though it's just March. So warm that this afternoon, Miles has been outside mowing and doing yardwork shirtless. And I have been watching him from the window with a strong urge to run my palms over his muscular arms, over his tattoos and down his chest. So strong that I've been taking Blackjack out more often than needed for potty breaks to get a closer look.

I actually want to be with my husband again.

And he doesn't want me.

That's why I decide I need a distraction. A road trip to see my parents would work, maybe get my mind from constantly thinking about sex.

When Miles comes in and grabs a beer from the refrigerator, sadly with his shirt back on, I run my idea past him.

"I was thinking about taking a trip down to see my parents since I haven't seen them in a month. They can meet Blackjack," I tell him while resting my forearms on the bar counter.

"When?" is his grunted one-word response between gulps of his beer.

"Whenever. Maybe tomorrow?"

"Fine," he mutters. Then he tosses his beer into the trash can and stomps off to the bathroom.

Great.

Does he not want me to go?

Did he want to come too?

How am I supposed to know what he's thinking or what he wants if grunts are his preferred method of communication?

CHAPTER EIGHTEEN

Miles

I KNEW Kira was planning to head out to see her folks today, but the rolling luggage is a complete surprise.

"You're staying overnight?" I snap at her because I had assumed, apparently wrongly, that she would go down this morning and come back tonight.

"Ah, yeah. Is that not okay?" Kira asks, picking up Jack and cuddling him like he's her safety blanket. Whenever I'm around her, she's holding the damn dog. And yeah, I'll admit he's a cute little bastard, but fuck!

It's been four weeks since Kira and I got married.

Four weeks since I fucked her.

Hell, four weeks since the last time I touched her, which is why I'm jealous of the damn mutt. That little fucker gets to lick her face constantly.

"You like the dog better than me," I state as a fact, not a question.

"I...what?" she asks.

"Not taking him with you probably never crossed your mind," I say, angry that she didn't care to invite me along. She's going to visit her parents *overnight* to get away from me.

"My parents haven't seen him yet..." she replies.

"Why don't you just pack up the rest of your shit and not come back," I snap at her, reaching the breaking point of my patience and sexual frustration.

Her jaw drops and then her eyes turn glassy when she asks, "You don't want me here?"

"I'm not holding you hostage even though you act like I am!" I yell at her. "Hell, I'll even help you get everything down to your car to make it easier on you," I tell her when I go and pick up the handle on her luggage and start for the door.

"What? No, wait!" Kira yells, and then she's blocking the door, her hands empty of the dog for once since she must have put him in his pen.

"You don't want to be here," I say through clenched teeth. "You flinch away from me, and I haven't even tried to touch you since the first night!"

"Then try," she says. "And I'll...I'll try not to flinch."

A sound of non-humorous laughter leaves my mouth. "No, thanks, princess. I may be a killer, but rape's not really my thing."

"I-I want to be with you again," she stammers, and I know she's full of shit. Why she's lying I have no clue.

Except for one reason.

"You just want to stick around to make sure I don't get a refund," I say in understanding. "What the hell did you want all that money for anyway? You don't ever buy anything unless I make you."

"Please don't send me home," she begs, her big, pleading, blue eyes giving the mutt a run for his money. "I'll do whatever you want me to do. I'll sleep with you. It'll be good. I can get better at all of this, I swear."

What the fuck is she talking about? She thought the night we were together wasn't good?

"You ran away from me last time telling me not to touch you, remember?" I remind her.

"I-I'll make it up to you," she says. "Right now."

Before I can respond to that, she's sinking down on her knees in front of me.

"Kira, what the hell are you doing?" I ask when her shaking hands try to undo my belt buckle.

"I've never given a, um, a blowjob before," she informs me while she works on unfastening my pants. "But I'm a fast learner."

"You don't have to do this," I tell her, glancing down to watch as her trembling fingers lower my zipper. "Go home. Fuck the money–" My protests are abruptly cut off when she wraps her fingers around my cock and the crown slips past her plump red lips.

She's so damn sexy with my dick in her mouth, until her cheeks puff out which is equal parts adorable and hilarious. I know I'm an enormous jackass for chuckling, but I can't seem to help myself.

When her confused blue eyes lift to my face, I can't keep a straight face when I tell her, "You don't actually blow on it, princess. You suck it. *Oh, fuck!*" I groan when she quickly starts to apply suction. "You are a fast learner," I say while propping my forearms on the door to rest my forehead on them to watch her, preventing me from touching her until she says the words.

Kira

I'm an idiot.

But I refuse to give up. I can make Miles feel as good as he made me feel if he gives me a chance.

101

And he does.

As if aware of my jaw getting sore from trying to take all of his length, he provides me with further instruction.

"You can use your hand if you want. Oh, hell yeah, just like that," he responds when I wrap my fingers around his slick cock and stroke it up and down. "Licking feels nice too," he adds, so I rub the tip of his cock over the flat of my tongue. "My boys like some hand and mouth attention too."

Since I'm assuming he's referring to his balls, I lift his cock straight up to run my tongue over the thin skin covering his sack before taking one into my mouth.

"God, yes, Kira," Miles grunts above me, throwing his head back for several seconds before he rests his forehead on his arms again to keep watching me. "Suck my cock again. I want to see it fucking your mouth."

Since I want to please him, I open wide and let him thrust his shaft inside until I gag and he pulls back.

"You can take more, princess," Miles says confidently. I take him to the back of my throat and then swallow as he starts to retreat. "Fuck, yeah. Your pouty lips and virgin mouth were made to suck cock. Oh Jesus Christ!" he shouts as his hips pump in and out faster and faster.

My hands that are wrapped around Miles' thighs feel them start to tremble while his curses turn into animalistic growls.

"You want me to come down your throat?" it sounds like he asks, but it's hard to tell since his voice is so deep and gruff.

My eyes lock with his as I give a slight nod of agreement.

"*FUCK!*" he roars as his hot seed explodes in my mouth.

I'm taking everything he gives me, even though his orgasm seems to go on forever. I'm pretty proud of myself since this is my first time.

But then all of a sudden, my stomach heaves without warning. I start to gag again, and Miles pulls his shaft out of my mouth just in time for me to throw up on the floor and even the toes of his boots.

Mortified beyond belief, I slap my hand over my mouth as if that will do any good now.

Neither of us say a word or move for several long seconds.

Finally Miles takes a step backward and pulls up his pants. I still can't lift my eyes to his yet.

"Clean this shit up," he says as I hear his zipper. He doesn't even fasten his belt buckle before he pushes the door open and steps over me.

"Oh my god. What have I done?" I ask the empty room.

I was supposed to be showing Miles that I want him, that I want to stay so he won't ask for half of his money back that my parents need, and now he must hate me for getting sick on him after doing...that.

Now he'll send me away for sure!

CHAPTER NINETEEN

Miles

GUESS THAT ANSWERS MY QUESTION – Kira thinks I'm disgusting.

In all my life, I've never had a woman do...*that* afterward. And I didn't even lay a hand on her! I didn't force her to suck my dick or swallow! She insisted, and then...fuck me.

That's it. She's got to go back home. I can't live in the same house knowing how fucking amazing it feels to be inside of her while at the same time being well aware of the fact that Kira apparently despises me.

From now on, I'll sleep at the clubhouse until she takes the hint and leaves. I meant what I said. Fuck the money. She can keep it. I think she's earned it after this morning.

When I get to the Savage Asylum, I stick my head in the chapel where Torin is going through stacks of paperwork like usual, although he's been putting in fewer hours now that he's married and has a family.

"Mind if I crash in an apartment for a while?" I ask him.

Looking up, our president lifts one dirty blond eyebrow and says, "I didn't know you weren't staying in the apartment."

"Oh. Right. Long story," I mutter.

"Everything okay?" he asks. Then his nose wrinkles. "Why do you smell like vomit?"

"Shit. Sorry," I reply with a wince. "I need to try and clean my boots off."

"How did you get vomit on your boots? Do I even want to know the answer to that question?"

"No, probably not," I say and start to walk away before turning back to him. "Have you ever had a woman...get sick after blowing you?" Even saying the word *blow* reminds me of how damn cute and innocent Kira was trying to get me off. Before she got sick.

"Ah, yeah. It happens," Torin responds with a shrug when he goes back to his stack of papers.

"Seriously?" I ask. "You're not just saying that to make me feel better?"

"Do you think I would say shit ever to spare your feelings?" he grumbles without glancing up.

"No."

"Then trust me when I say it happens. Not often, but it does," he replies before a grin spreads across his face. "When Lexi was pregnant with Kenzi, she tossed her cookies almost every time we fooled around. It was so awful that I even begged her to wait a few weeks, but she was so horny that it wasn't an option either. We had to start fucking in the bathroom so she could barf right after we finished."

"Really? You made Lexi sick?"

"No, asshole. It was the pregnancy, morning sickness that happened all day. I even asked the doctor about it, and he said some women do that shit for whatever reason after sex. Thankfully it stopped in the second trimester. I was starting to worry that it was me repulsing her, but it turns out it was just the hormones or whatever those first few weeks."

While I stand there staring at Torin without blinking and trying to let that information sink in, I'm pretty sure all the blood drains from my face because I start to feel a little dizzy.

"Did you knock someone up?" Torin snaps when he glances back up at me.

"I don't know," I mutter before I turn around and leave, needing some time to think this through.

Could Kira be pregnant? Am I gonna be a fucking father?

We were only together that one time!

Was she with someone else before we got married? If so, I'll put a bullet in that son of a bitch!

Kira

AFTER I CLEAN up the embarrassing mess I made, I call my mom to let her know I'm getting ready to leave. The sooner I leave this place to escape the humiliation, the better.

My mom doesn't answer at home or at the warehouse, so I try her cell phone.

"Hello," my mother's voice answers, and I know right away that something is wrong. She sounds stuffy, like she has a cold, or she's been crying.

"Mom, are you okay?" I ask.

"Kira," she says with a sniffle. "It's your father..."

"Oh, god. What happened?" I ask as my chest tightens with worry.

"Zeno –" she starts.

"Zeno? Why is Zeno bothering him? You paid him all the money back weeks ago!"

"Kozlov sent him back last night, wanted him to find out where we got so much money so fast!" she explains. "And your father feels so awful, but he couldn't take anymore!"

"Anymore what? What happened, Mom?"

"They kept hitting him! His face is a mess, and he won't let me take him to the hospital!"

"Jesus, Mom! I'm on my way!" I tell her.

"No! Don't come here. We're leaving. It's not safe to stay!"

"Then where are you going? I'll meet you there," I assure her.

"You need to warn Miles," she says. "They could be coming for him. Both of you need to get out of town!"

"Miles? What do you mean?"

"Your father gave them his name as the source of the money. It was the only way he could stay alive!"

"Oh, my god," I mutter in understanding. The Russians beat my father to find out how he came up with all the money he owed them so fast without selling the house. They must have thought he was skimming off of them or had more earnings they didn't know about. If he told them Miles paid half a million to marry me, they'll think he's an easy target to shake down for more money.

I know Miles can take care of himself, but not against a group of armed thugs!

"I need to pack," my mom tells me. "I'll call you when we're someplace safe. You do the same."

"Okay," I agree. "I love you. Tell Daddy I'm sorry and I love him too."

"We love you, Kira. Stay safe," she says in a rush before the line goes dead.

I slump down onto the sofa with the phone still in my hand, trying to decide what to do.

Miles is probably so angry at me from earlier that he'll go ballistic when I tell him about the Russians.

But I need to tell him the truth and get out of town like my mother suggested.

I just hope he'll listen to me and forgive me.

CHAPTER TWENTY

Miles

I'm surprised to see Kira's car is still in the driveway when I pull up on my bike. I thought she would be long gone by now, so it's a relief to see that she didn't bolt.

Now I just have to figure out how to ask her if she could be pregnant, and if so, who the fuck is the father.

As soon as I walk in the door, she jumps up from the sofa and swipes her fingers under her eyes.

Great. She's been crying again.

Not only do I make her sick, I make her sad. I can't figure out which is worse.

"Kira, we need to talk," I say, leaning my back against the closed front door and crossing my arms over my chest.

"Yes, we do," she says. "I'm so, so sorry about this morning, but I'm even more sorry about dragging you into my parents' mess!"

Her arms are hugging herself tightly, and it's obvious from five feet away that she's also shaking.

"Hold on. What?" I ask, pushing off the door to go to her.

"They hurt my dad and-and made him tell them your name! I need to go see him, but my mom said I should stay away. I don't know what to do!"

"Calm down and start from the beginning," I instruct.

I go over and sit on one end of the sofa, also known as her bed, hoping she'll follow. She does, taking a seat on the other end, pulling up her knees to her chest and wrapping her arms around them.

"Okay, so my dad owed a man a lot of money," she starts. The words hits me like a brick wall out of nowhere.

"That's why you needed half a million!" I exclaim in disbelief. "You *married* me to pay off your father's debt?"

"Yes."

"Jesus fucking Christ," I mutter as I pinch the top of my nose where a massive headache is starting.

This woman gave up her life to marry me just to save her father, and now she's knocked up with my kid, or someone else's. I thought she wanted the money for herself, but it's been weeks and she's only bought the shit I make her, like food and supplies for the dog.

"It's fine, I didn't mind helping him," she says.

"Giving up your life for a strange man to settle your dad's debt is not fucking fine," I tell her. "How could he even ask you do to that?"

"It *is* fine. And he didn't ask me. I did it without them knowing because I love my parents. I would do anything for them," Kira replies, which is pretty damn admirable even though what she did is a little insane. "But then after all the money was paid, they came back wanting to know where my father made that much money so fast. My mom said his face is-is messed up from where they hit him over and over until he told them everything, about the wedding, the money and...you."

"Your old man okay?" I ask, throwing my arm over the back of the sofa when the stupid appendage tries to reach out and touch her, to soothe her. Haven't I learned anything after this morning? She doesn't want me. She only married me out of an obligation to her folks, not to try and make things work with me as my wife.

"Yes, he's going to be okay. But you may not be! If Zeno shows up here looking for easy money, he won't take no for an answer!"

Holy shit.

Is she worried about me?

Or is she worried she could get caught in the middle?

"I won't let them hurt you," I assure her. "That's a fucking promise."

"These men are...rough. And dangerous. Zeno won't be alone, so it'll be you against several of them!"

"I can take care of myself," I assure her. "Everything is going to be fine."

"You don't understand," she says with a shake of her head. "I know you can take on one or even two or three, but these guys carry guns! We should probably leave..."

"I have guns too, and I can fucking guarantee you that I'm a better shot than they are," I explain. When her blue eyes still look skeptical, I tell her, "Years ago, I was a Scout Sniper for the Marines."

"You were in the military?" Kira asks, brows raising with interest as she rests her chin on her knees.

"It was a long time ago, and I'm a different man now," I respond. "But I'm still an expert with a rifle or any other gun in my hands." Getting to my feet and starting for the kitchen, I tell her, "Come here."

Kira gets up and walks over. When she's close enough to see, I open the second bottom cabinet and remove the Smith & Wesson that's fastened to the top. "If I'm not around and someone comes to the door, you can grab this one, if you know how to use it."

Giving a small nod, she says, "I do. My father has guns."

"Okay, good," I say in surprise before putting the gun back. "There's also one under my side of the mattress and one under the bathroom sink. Just don't use them on me," I warn her. "If you want to leave, then leave."

Leaning her hip against the counter, she asks, "Do you want me to go?"

"I'm not forcing you to stay here."

"That's not what I asked," Kira says. "Do you *want* me to go?"

"No," I admit without hesitation.

Her eyes lower to where her fingernail starts to pick at the edge of the counter top. "You say you don't, but it would be nice if you could show me too."

"Show you?" I repeat in confusion.

"Yes," she replies.

"How am I supposed to show you?"

"You don't ever...touch me."

"Touch you? You told me not to touch you, so I haven't!"

Her blue eyes come up to mine, wide in shock. "That's why you haven't..." she trails off.

"I'm not going to make you do anything."

"I want you to touch me again," she says softly, which is fucking mind-blowing to hear since I was certain she couldn't stand me.

"You sure about that?" I ask, unable to take her statement at face value. Not when everything she's said and done over the last few weeks contradicts it. "If you lock yourself in the bathroom and cry again afterward, we're done," I tell her honestly. "I'll pack your shit up and take you home myself."

"I won't," she says. "That first day was just...intense."

"Yeah, I've been criticized for that before," I grumble.

"It's not a bad thing. I just haven't been with many men."

"How many?" I ask.

"Three. Counting you," she says, avoiding eye contact with me again which gives my eyes a chance to drink in the rest of her body that's close enough to touch. Her perky tits are looking fuller than usual, hard nipples pointing right at me through her top. Her dark jeans are so snug on her long legs that I can almost make out her pussy lips in the crotch.

"How many times did you fuck the other two?" I question her because I'm happy she's talking to me. I would enjoy the subject more if we weren't talking about her sexual history with two other assholes.

"Seven times."

"Wow," I mutter. I wouldn't have expected a young, beautiful, sexy girl like Kira to have been with a ton of guys before, but she looks like the long-term girlfriend type who would gladly spread her legs for her boyfriend whenever he wanted it.

"When was the last time? Before me?" I ask curiously, for more than one reason.

"A few years ago," she answers, which means that, if she is knocked up, the kid is mine.

Fuck.

"So, I don't know how to do to you what you did to me that night..." she says, blue eyes framed with long, dark lashes locked on mine.

Jesus, she's gorgeous. And she could be carrying a part of me inside of her right fucking now.

"Yeah, you do know how," I assure her, glancing down at her belly to see if it looks any different. It's hard to tell through her shirt. I'd love to get my hands underneath it to find out for sure.

"No, I don't," she argues.

"This morning you did just fucking fine. Well, before you..."

"Really?" she asks with a hint of a smile lifting her naughty girl lips.

"Yeah," I tell her. Which reminds me that I really need to find out if she's late or whatever. "And, ah, about that, what happened this morning..."

"Could you maybe give me some pointers in bed? Teach me to be better for you?" she asks, causing all the blood in my body to rush south faster than ever before.

Fuck talking.

We can talk later.

"You don't need to try to be better for me," I tell her.

"Oh. Okay," she says, actually sounding disappointed.

"It's impossible because you're already fucking incredible," I say when I close the distance between us to grab her hip, sliding my thumb underneath her shirt to touch her soft skin.

CHAPTER TWENTY-ONE

Kira

Oh, god. He's touching me again.

It's no more than the pad of his thumb on my hip, but to my libido you would think he ripped my clothes off.

I really wish he would rip my clothes off.

"Could I –" I try to say but a gasp interrupts when his thumb dips into my waistband.

"Could you what?" Miles asks, his gruff voice even deeper, his face just inches away from mine.

"Could I...maybe sleep with you tonight?" I finally blurt out the rest of my question for him.

His grip tightens on my hip while the fingers on his other hand come up to tug on the top button of my jeans, undoing them. "We need to work on our communication. No more jumping to the wrong conclusions and making assumptions," he says. "What do you imagine we'll be doing in my bed when you sleep with me tonight?" he asks while lowering my zipper.

"You'll touch me?"

"Is that a question or a request?" he demands brusquely.

"Both."

"Fuck, yes, I'm going to touch you," Miles growls. His hand on my hip starts gliding slowly north, up my waist, stopping so that his thumb can rub circles over my beaded nipple, causing my breath to shudder. "What else?"

"Kiss me."

"You want me to kiss you?" he asks, stilling his thumb.

"Yes," I reply. "And..."

"And what?" Miles asks as he jerks my shirt over my head and throws it behind him. His eyes are lowered to my breasts that feel heavier all of a sudden, like they're heaving out of the cups of my teal-colored bra.

"And not just my mouth." The words barely leave my mouth before Miles hits his knees. He leans forward and his tongue flicks in and out of my belly button, simulating how he licked me lower before.

When he stops, he looks up at me with his palms on my ass, squeezing and then pulling my jeans down my legs. "Show me where you want me to kiss you." Before I can speak, he growls and then his teeth scrape over my lower belly, biting at the waistband of my matching teal thong, making me give an embarrassing squeal. He drags the satin toward the floor, rubbing his nose down my pelvis and burying it in the apex of my thighs.

God, it feels so naughty to be standing in the kitchen nearly naked in just my bra with my pants around my knees, his face pressed to my crotch.

But it's exactly what I've been wanting since that first night.

"There...I want you to kiss me there," I tell him, placing my hands on his shoulders for balance when my legs go weak. "And I don't want you to stop until I..."

"Until you come on my tongue?" Miles finishes right before the tip of his tongue spears my flesh.

"*Yesss*," I moan as my eyes slam closed and my head falls back.

Without his tongue pausing, Miles grabs one of my hands on his shoulder and places it on the side of his head.

Later I may even be embarrassed by how hard I pressed his face to my body, but right now it feels too good to care.

When the pleasure starts to build, I worry Miles will stop, leaving me on the precipice over and over again like before. So I cradle his head in both of my hands to keep him in place until the dam inside of me bursts wide open.

"Oh god, oh god, oh god!" I chant until my words turn into gasps, followed by an open-mouthed silent scream to the heavens.

The world tilts as I begin to come back down, and then I realize I'm sitting on the kitchen counter, still clutching Miles' head while he removes my snug jeans the rest of the way down my legs and off.

"Why didn't you tell me you needed my tongue in your pussy again?" he asks with his lips on the inside of my thighs. "I would've been eating you out all three meals every day."

"I-I thought you didn't want me," I whisper, still floating down from my lust high.

"You have no idea how much I want you, princess," he replies.

His words make me smile, but then I'm slapping my palm over my mouth when the same violent twist from this morning happens in my stomach.

"Oh shit," Miles says, scrambling to his feet. He reaches for the dish rag on the sink and wets it while all I can do is sit there para-lyzed from the sudden onset of nausea.

"Just breathe," he tells me when he places the rag on the back of my neck and holds it there. "In through your nose, out through your mouth slowly. Try to think about something else, and maybe it'll pass."

I nod quickly, hoping he's right. Since Miles is so close to me, still holding the rag to me, I grab his shoulders and bury my face in his neck to inhale his intoxicating scent. He smells like the leather of his vest mixed with his spicy, masculine aftershave.

After just a few deep breaths, my stomach seems to settle down.

"You smell good," I tell him.

"Sniffing me helps?" he asks.

"Yes. I think so."

"Good."

When I start to pull back, Miles turns his head and then his lips are on mine, kissing me for the very first time. He sucks on my bottom lip before saying, "Stop me if you feel sick again."

"Okay," I agree before putting my hands on his neck to bring his mouth back down to mine. His hard body wedges between my bare legs, grinding the bulging fly of his jeans right against my clit.

"Pull my cock out so I can feel you," he orders, so I fumble with his zipper while his tongue slides along mine. I taste myself on him, but it just turns me on even more.

When I wrap my fingers around his long, firm shaft to pull him free, Miles groans into my mouth. And when I rub his blunt tip through my slit, he breaks our kiss to shout out a curse.

I love that I affect him this way, that just the barest touch makes him as hot as it makes me.

The rag on the back of my neck falls, and then Miles is frantically digging through his jean pocket and pulling out a condom. He has the foil packet open and his shaft sheathed in record breaking time.

Then his hands go under my knees, lifting them off the counter and spreading my thighs wide to open me up for him. One hard shove forward and he's filling me to the hilt.

I'm still gasping from the first thrust when he picks me up off the counter and then starts slamming me down on his cock. I wrap an arm around his neck to hold on as he fucks me hard and fast. He's so deep I swear I can feel him in my belly.

∼

Miles

I TOLD myself I was going to go slow if Kira ever let me inside of her again, but fuck if I could hold back once she rubbed my cock on her wet pussy.

God, I wanted to feel every slick inch of her. She may not be pregnant, though. Her upchuck reflex could just all be caused by me. If so, I don't want to take another chance with her, so I put on the goddamn condom.

It's impossible for me to get deep enough. Not when she was on the counter, or when I picked her up. I eventually lay her down on the middle of the kitchen floor. With her knees pressed to her tits, I finally hit rock bottom. Or heaven, as it should be called.

And she wanted me to kiss her, but it's impossible right now. I swear I will after I get us both off. I'll take her to bed and kiss her lips and lick her pussy for the rest of the night as soon as her pussy clamps down on my cock and milks me dry.

I jerk the cups of her bra down to get both of my hands on her tits to give them a squeeze while I thrust mercilessly.

When Kira cries out, I worry I've gone too far.

"Did I hurt you?" I still long enough to ask and get a response.

"No! Don't stop!" she exclaims, reaching around to grab my ass cheeks, digging in her fingernails to pull me toward her body. "I'm so close...it hurts."

"Hold on, princess," I tell her, bracing one palm on the dishwasher behind her head. I slip my other hand under her ass to tilt her hips up and hammer inside of her body until finally, finally her cunt puts my cock in a vise grip and she screams my name.

And fuck, it's like a fantasy come true seeing her beautiful face go slack with pleasure as my release races down my spine and tightens my balls before exploding in hot pulses from my cock.

"Fuck, Kira. *Fuck!*" I shout through the body-wracking tremors that leave me feeling weak, like all my limbs have turned into liquid.

I sit back on my heels to keep from crushing my girl, especially if she's pregnant, while I recover, letting her lower her knees back down.

"That was...exactly what I needed," Kira says when my pants are nearly gone. Then, her palms ease under my shirt and her fingertips stroke my stomach. "Why didn't you get naked with me?"

"No need to," I reply, pulling her hands back out even though I immediately miss them.

"You have a really nice body," she says while I peel off the condom and toss it in the trash under the sink, then zip up my jeans. "I saw you mowing without a shirt the other day."

Shit.

"What do all of your tattoos mean?"

"Nothing," I reply when I'm on my feet, because there's no way I'm telling her what all the birds symbolize. If she's not sick yet, they'll make her nauseous. "You feeling okay?"

"Yeah."

"Are you on birth control?" I blurt out.

"No. Why? You used a condom, right?" she asks when she sits up.

"Yeah, I did. But last time..." I start to say and stop when I hear footsteps on the wooden steps outside.

"What?" Kira asks, but I crouch down and slap my hand over her mouth to listen closer, causing her eyes to bug out. But then she hears it too, the wood creaking; and her confusion turns to fear.

"Shh," I whisper when I let go of her mouth to reach over and as quietly as possible remove the Smith & Wesson from the cabinet.

None of my brothers know I bought a house, so they definitely don't know the address. The paperwork was filed weeks ago, so it's on the public record. All someone would have to do to find me is look it up.

I never thought it would be a problem until Kira told me about the shit with her parents.

Well, there's one way to tell if the incoming is friendly or antagonistic. Friends knock.

I quickly check the clip and rack the slide, putting a bullet in the chamber right as something heavy slams against the door, making Blackjack start to bark.

Whoever it is plans to come in with force.

The situation is not ideal, with Kira naked except for her bra on the floor beside me, but the bar provides pretty good cover. They'll never suspect I'll be armed and crouching.

That's why I don't move when I hear the door splinter apart at the lock.

No, I wait until I hear footsteps enter and hear a man say, "Check the bedrooms," before I pop up and hold my breath while firing four quick shots, one in each man's temple. They collapse to the floor like puppets having their strings clipped. If they're not dead, they will be within seconds, that's for certain.

When no other bodies step through the door, I glance over to check on Kira. She's huddled in the corner, knees to her chest and both of her palms slapped over her mouth. Her eyes are watering, but she's not freaking out.

"Good girl," I tell her while the puppy keeps barking. "Stay right there, okay?"

She gives a slight nod of her head, so I slip out from behind the counter, check the porch and then the driveway. There's no one else lurking, but I still go and open up the doors of the black Hummer blocking my driveway to check for more passengers, even the cargo area. It's thankfully empty.

When I see old man Reynolds checking his mail, I hold up the gun and yell, "Fucking squirrels" just in case his ancient ears heard the shots being fired.

His eyes narrow at the mention of the critters he hates.

"You get a new ride?" he calls back to me.

"Test driving," I reply. "It's too big. I think I'll look for something smaller."

"Gas guzzlers," he says with a shake of his head before he goes back into his house.

The rest of the neighborhood looks clear, not many cars in driveways since it's the afternoon and most people are still working.

Jogging back up the steps, I pull the door closed even though it won't lock and check on Kira.

"All clear," I tell her. "I'll clean this mess up when it gets dark," I promise her with a wave of my hand toward the area of dead men. "You can take Blackjack and wait in the bedroom if you want. Or I can take you someplace safe."

"No. I'll stay," she says when I offer her a hand up and she starts locating her clothing to get dressed, starting with her panties and jeans.

"You sure, princess?" I ask, and she nods as her shirt goes over her head. "Just don't look –" I start to say, but she's already walking around me, going to the dog's pen to pick him up. While she's clutching him in her arms, petting his head furiously, she looks at the men.

"That's Zeno," she whispers. "I don't recognize the others."

"Zeno, the guy your dad owed money to?" I ask.

"Yes. Well, no," she huffs. "I need to take Jack outside."

"I'll come with you," I tell her when she goes to the door and slips on her shoes. I figure fresh air will be good to help calm her down after seeing me kill four men. Not that she seems all that shook up right now.

It's probably shock.

In a few minutes or hours, she'll realize what I've done and never let me lay a hand on her again.

How fucking ironic since I just finally got to be with her after waiting and wanting her for weeks?

Marriage is torture.

I'm tied to her, no matter if she's scared to death of me. I should let her go, but it seems impossible now, even though we've only been together a short time.

In the backyard, Blackjack hops along the sparse grass thanks to the sandy terrain, raising his leg to pee on the fence every two feet, marking his territory and yipping at the air like he's a tough guy expecting more visitors.

"Tell me about Zeno," I say to Kira, figuring it'll be easier to get her talking out here.

"He works for a man who helped my father start up his furniture business thirty years ago," she says. "A man in Russia who uses his wood and fabric shipments to import illegal things into the country."

"What kind of illegal things?"

"I'm not entirely sure, but I think it's guns and drugs."

"So why did your dad owe him so much money?"

"There was a fire a few months ago. His furniture warehouse burned down, along with the things my dad was storing for Kozlov."

"And Kozlov's the guy back in Russia?" I ask.

"Yes. Zeno comes over to the states every so often to check in on their business interests, taking a percentage of profits from my dad and other people he helped get started here. Most of the conversations about Zeno and Kozlov are in Russian between my parents. I think I've heard them use the word for second, like Zeno is next in line to take over since he handles all the finances."

"Next in line to take what over?"

"The, ah, the Russian mafia," she says while fidgeting with the hem of her shirt. "That's bad, right?"

A choked cough is the only sound I can make after hearing that news flash.

I just killed four men...in the Russian mafia.

Mafias aren't much different from MCs like the Savage Kings. If you fuck with one member, you get fucked up by them all.

It may be a while before news of Zeno's demise gets back to the big daddy Russian; but when it does, we're going to be screwed.

We meaning me, Kira, her parents...and now the Savage Kings.

If those men knew my name, they could easily find out about my association with the Kings and come after the whole club.

I need to fill in the guys, let them know about this clusterfuck I've inadvertently caused so we can start doing damage control.

First thing first, I need to get rid of four bodies.

At least they were kind enough to leave me with the perfect mode of transportation.

CHAPTER TWENTY-TWO

Kira

THE AFTERNOON HAS BEEN INCREDIBLY surreal.

One minute I'm freaking out about Zeno coming after Miles. The next Miles and I are going at it, having earth-shattering sex, and then he's killing Zeno and three other guys in the blink of an eye.

None of the men who barged into his house even fired a single shot. That's how fast Miles took them down. I knew he was tough, and he told me about his sniper experience in the Marines, but seeing him in action, looking so badass is a whole other thing.

The fact that my husband can kill men so efficiently shouldn't be hot, should it?

And this afternoon is the first time that I've looked at him and thought of him as just that, my husband.

The last few weeks he's just been a stranger I happen to live in the same house with, occasionally talk to and hooked up with once.

Now, things have changed.

He said he wants me.

He *showed* me he wants me.

It feels like something has shifted between us, like we're closer after the sex.

Or the murders.

I'm not sure which.

So when night falls and Miles takes off his leather vest to put on a black hoodie, a baseball hat and black leather gloves, I find myself telling him, "I can help you."

"Help me what?" he asks absently as he pulls on the second glove.

"Get rid of them."

He pauses with his hand in the air to lock eyes with me. "Are you offering to help me dispose of four dead men?"

"Yes."

"Why?"

"You can't move them on your own, can you?" I ask.

"Like hell I can't."

"But wouldn't it be easier if I helped? You know, like carrying their feet."

Gloved hands going to his hips, he says, "Why aren't you freaking the fuck out? I killed four guys."

"I know," I reply. "And I'm glad they're dead. Well, I'm glad Zeno is dead. I didn't know the others, but they were probably assholes like him. Is that an awful thing to say? I'm a horrible person."

"No, you're not," Miles says. "I'm a bad person. You, on the other hand, are...perfect."

"So are you going to let me help you or not?"

"You sure about this?" he asks.

"Yes."

"All right," he agrees.

"So what's the plan?"

Miles just stares at me again before eventually answering my questions. "First, we need to roll them up in plastic; then we'll take each one to the Hummer and load them up. I'll take them to Hull Swamp and dump them. The water's deep enough and dirty enough to hide them until something comes along and makes them disappear."

"Okay. Let's get this over with," I tell him as I glance over to the gross men still bleeding out on the towels Miles laid on our floor.

Our floor.

I'm so used to referring to the house as Miles' that I'm not sure when it became ours.

Maybe after he fucked my brains out in *our* kitchen.

Sex with Miles is addictive. He's addictive. I want more of him. And I feel safe with him, protected.

"Have you killed other men before?" I ask him. He's so calm about this, I get the feeling he's done it a time or two.

"Yes."

"How many?"

"Less talking, more working," he says, rolling out black plastic.

He doesn't want to tell me, and I'm not sure why not.

Just like I can't figure out why he didn't take his shirt and pants off when we were going at it earlier.

The next time we have sex, I want to feel his skin against mine and run my fingers over his sexy, bad boy tattoos.

But first, we have bodies to get rid of.

Dead men are heavy. Especially Zeno, the jerk. He had to weigh more than two hundred pounds.

"I can't wait to come back and go to bed," I say once the last man is loaded up in the back of the Hummer.

"We won't be back until late," Miles says. "After we dump them, we have to dispose of the SUV."

"Oh, crap."

"And first, we need to go back inside and clean up the blood."

Yuck.

Apparently, killing bad guys is the easy part. Getting rid of them and all the evidence is a serious pain in the butt.

CHAPTER TWENTY-THREE

Miles

NEVER IN MY life did I expect a good girl like Kira to help me dispose of these fuckers.

I could've managed on my own, but it was nice to have a little help. We got it done faster with teamwork.

My wife and I are pretty damn good at moving dead bodies.

And everything is going great until we get to the swamp.

I open up the back hatch while wincing at the foul smell the four corpses are producing. It occurs to me that I should have warned her they're going to start smelling fast, just as I hear Kira heave.

No. Fuck no.

"Get back in the car," I tell her. But then I hear her hand hitting the side of the Hummer as she bends over. "No, no, no, princess," I tell her, lifting the hair from the back of her neck to cool her down. "You can't get sick out here. We don't want any of our DNA left with their DNA. Got it?" I ask. "Breathe in through your nose, out through the mouth. You can beat this shit down, baby."

She nods her head and pulls her shirt up over her nose and mouth.

"That's good. Block out the smell and calm your stomach before you go sit down."

"I'm okay. I'm okay," she says when she turns to face me, assuring me or herself, I'm not sure which.

I wonder if she'll say that after she finds out she's pregnant.

If she actually is.

Only one way to find out.

And I need to tell her soon so that we can get a test to be sure.

Is it wrong that I hope she is because it means I'll get to keep her?

But what if she's upset and angry if the test is positive and blames me? I can't make her stay with me. Well, technically I could, but I won't.

All she was trying to do was help her father get out of a mess, not tie herself to an asshole killer like me.

Kira

"I'm so sorry I put you through all of this," Miles says when we pull away from the swamp.

"No. It's my father's fault. And I swear I don't usually have such a weak stomach. Normally, it takes a lot to make me queasy, but today has been awful. Maybe I've got a stomach bug or something."

"Ah, about that," he starts, glancing quickly at me in the dark vehicle before his eyes turn to the road. "Are you late?"

"Late? Late for what, bed?" I ask in confusion before I yawn and rest my head on the cool glass of the window. The exhaustion of the exciting day is catching up with me.

"I think we need to get you a pregnancy test in the morning."

"*A what?*" I exclaim as I pop up straight again thanks to the surge of adrenaline pumping through my veins.

"A pregnancy test," Miles repeats the foreign words again. "Don't you think it's possible you could be pregnant?"

"No!" I shout. "How could I be pregnant? We've only slept together twice and once was today. Besides, you wore a condom both times."

The silence coming from Miles' side of the SUV is concerning.

"You-you did wear a condom the first time, right?" I ask. The question is followed by only crickets chirping while I try to figure out today's date and count the weeks backward in my head. "Miles?"

"*Do it! Do it now!*" he finally says.

"What does that mean?"

"That's what you said when we were fucking, and I told you I wanted to come inside of you. I thought you were on birth control pills!"

"I thought you were wearing a condom!" I yell back at him.

"Are you kidding me, right now?" he huffs. "Then why would my cum be dripping down your thighs afterward if I had on a condom?" he snaps back at me. "Fucking with a rubber doesn't feel that damn good or cause that big of a mess."

"I just...I just figured it was all from where I, ah, enjoyed myself," I admit. "The guys I've been with always used condoms and I never had an orgasm with them, so I didn't know!" I shout at him when the last date of my period finally pops into my head. "Oh, my god. It's been seven or eight weeks! I-I could be...pregnant," I whisper placing my hand on my belly when the reality of that word hits me, and tears overflow from my eyes.

"I'm sorry, Kira," Miles says. "I shouldn't have done that...but I don't regret it. I hope you won't either. I'll even understand if you don't want to keep it..."

"Why...why wouldn't I keep it?"

"Because we didn't mean for this to happen. And it's my fault for putting this on you," he explains. "I don't want you to feel trapped, with me or the kid."

"So-so you-you don't want it?" I stammer between the sniffles.

"Fuck, don't cry, princess," Miles says, and then his palm hits the steering wheel so hard I jump. "Look, this is your decision, okay? If you want to keep the kid, I'll make sure you both have everything you need. And if you don't want to keep it, I'll go with you to the doctor. Let's just get a test in the morning to know for sure, and then you can think it over for a few days."

"I don't need to think it over," I tell him softly.

"Oh. All right." Clearing his throat, Miles goes on to say, "I don't blame you. Especially after everything that happened this afternoon. We spent the night scrubbing blood from the floors and walls and getting rid of bodies. Who in their right mind would want to have *my* bastard spawn?"

I may not know Miles very well, but it sounds like he wants me to have this baby and is convinced that I won't keep it.

"He won't be a bastard." The word *he* instantly makes me think of holding our tiny baby, wrapped in a blue blanket. It's not all that scary to imagine even if it is unexpected, to say the least.

"What?" Miles asks.

"He, or I guess it could be a she," I reply, not minding one bit if the blanket was pink instead of blue, and maybe there's a little pink bow in her dark hair too. "Whichever it is, it won't be a bastard. We were married before..."

"Oh, yeah, right," he mutters.

When he pulls up at the house, I say, "I thought we had to get rid of the SUV."

"Shit!" he huffs. "I forgot." Scrubbing both hands over his face, Miles says, "This will be easier. You can go pack your things."

"Why do I need to pack my things?" I ask him.

"'Cause more of them could be coming. I'll have to lay low until

132

this is all settled, and I'm guessing you would rather I take you back to your parents."

"Take me back to my parents?" I ask.

"I will. But it's late. Can't we do that tomorrow?"

"No, Miles," I reply. "I wasn't asking you to take me to them. I was trying to figure out what you mean by that statement."

"You can go. I won't ask for half of the money back," he says.

"I don't want to go back to my parents."

"Then where do you want to go?" he asks.

"Why do I have to go anywhere? I thought you said you wanted me to stay."

"I do," he responds. "But that was before I brought up the whole unplanned pregnancy shit or killed four fuckers!"

"I want to stay!"

"Really?" Miles asks, leaning his shoulder against the window to face me. In the glow of the streetlamps, I can see the surprise on his face.

"If we're gonna have a baby, then it should have a father in its life too."

"You're keeping it?"

"Yes."

"Are you sure, Kira? This is a lot more than you signed up for."

"And you didn't exactly sign up to have four men burst into your house to rob you either," I point out. "If you're not ready to get rid of me, then I'm staying. With you," I add to make it clear.

"You're staying, and you're gonna keep my kid?" he repeats as if he's not convinced.

"If I'm pregnant, then yes. Either way I don't want to leave."

"Why not?"

"Now you're asking me why I *don't* want to leave?"

"Yes. It just doesn't make sense," he grumbles.

"We're married," I remind him. "I didn't agree to this just for the money. I wanted a marriage. Besides, the sex is amazing too. Why would I want to walk away from that?"

"Get your ass inside and on the bed," Miles growls.

"What about getting rid of the SUV and packing?" I ask.

Reaching over, his gloved hand grabs a handful of my hair and tugs me forward so he can kiss my lips. Then, his wet, talented tongue moves lower, licking and sucking on the side of my neck before he says, "Tonight I'm taking my wife to bed and burying myself inside of her until the sun comes up. I'll kill anyone who tries to interrupt."

It's embarrassing how wet my panties get from a kiss on my neck and a few naughty words from my husband.

CHAPTER TWENTY-FOUR

Kira

"COME ON. We need to get dressed and pack up a few things," Miles says before the sun even starts to rise while running his fingers up and down my naked spine as we lay in bed.

"I'm so tired, though. Can't we sleep for a few hours?" I ask. He wasn't joking about being inside me all night. I enjoyed every second, although now I'm a little sore and incredibly exhausted.

"We can get some sleep when we're someplace with better security."

"What about Blackjack?" I ask.

"He's coming with us, so we need to grab his food and all too."

"Good."

"Now get moving," he says with a light slap to my bare bottom.

"This is so nice. I don't want to leave just yet," I tell him as I snuggle up to his chest, inhaling his spicy, masculine scent and letting my fingertips roam over his sexy abs. Not that I can see them in the dark, but I can feel them.

"Okay," Miles caves with a sigh. "Ten more minutes, then we have to get going."

"Thanks," I reply, placing a kiss on his smooth, warm stomach.

"The stores aren't open yet, but I'll get you a test as soon as I can."

"It's okay," I tell him because now I'm starting to already get attached to the possibility of a baby growing inside of me. Once I take a test, we'll know for certain. I'm not ready to have the possibility taken from me just yet if our assumption is wrong.

Although, even if I'm not pregnant yet, as many times as Miles came inside of me last night, he probably would've sealed the deal by now. I'm starting to wonder if that was his intention, because he was relentless, in the best way.

"The spare room could be a nursery," Miles says softly when he lifts my left hand to his lips and kisses my knuckles right above my wedding band.

"Yeah," I agree with a smile.

"I could've bought another bed and put it in there for you, but I was hoping you would eventually cave and come back to my bed if I made you sleep on the sofa."

"The sofa's comfortable," I tell him. "Not as comfortable as the bed, though. And I wasn't sure if you wanted me in it again."

"I was starting to think that I wouldn't ever get to have you in it again."

"Why wouldn't I?" I ask him. "You're kind and funny and sexy."

"If that's what you think, then you really don't know me," he mutters.

"Then let me get to know you," I reply.

"The lie is better than the reality."

"I doubt that."

"Trust me," he says before he slips out from underneath me and stands up to start getting dressed. I can barely make out more than his pale ass in the dark room, which is a shame.

"It hasn't been ten minutes."

"Close enough."

"Fine," I grumble. I'm so tired and was happy the way we were before he had to get all grouchy and jump ship. "Jack probably needs to go out anyway."

"I'll take him," Miles says. "You don't go outside on your own until this shit with the Russians is over. Do you understand?"

"Yes," I agree, unable to figure out if he's pissed at me for putting him in this situation or pissed off in general. Maybe he just needs some sleep too.

"I need to turn the light on," he says.

"Sure." Having some light should make it easier for me to locate all of my clothes that he threw around the room last night when we got home. Then I need to head for the shower.

Once my eyes adjust to the bright light, I watch Miles go over to the closet and then crouch down. There's an occasional beeping sound from the big, metal safe before he stands up and shoves a gun into the inside zipper of his vest. Or *cut*, I should say, after all the time's he's corrected me.

"Do you always carry a gun?" I ask him curiously.

"Yes. At least one."

"All the time? Even before all of this happened..."

"Always. Unless I'm naked," Miles responds. "Do you have anything of value I need to lock in the safe until I get the damn front door fixed?"

"No."

"Good. Don't leave any jewelry or cash in the house in case someone busts in."

"What about the television and the furniture?" I ask.

"It's all replaceable," he says simply before he walks out of the room.

"Yeah," I agree, finally climbing out of bed.

❦

HALF AN HOUR later and we're pulling up in a scrapyard-looking business with random trash and car parts lying around. The fact that the big lot is protected by a tall, barbed wire fence must be the reason why we're here.

With Blackjack in my arms, I throw my purse on my shoulder and climb out of the car just as a tall man with a limp comes out of one of the buildings.

"Miles? What's got you up and at it so early this morning?" the man asks.

"Need a favor. Mind if we crash here for a few hours?" Miles responds.

"Sure, sure."

"And I need you to crush this SUV ASAP."

"That's always a fun way to start the day. I'll do it right now," the man agrees as we meet him in the middle of the lot.

"Eddie, this is my wife Kira. Kira, this is Eddie," Miles says by way of introductions. I'm pretty sure it's only the second time I've ever heard him call me his wife.

"Hi. It's nice to meet you," I say when I shake the man's hand. His jaw is still gaping when I pull away.

"When did you get hitched? Do the guys know?"

"Ah, a few weeks ago, and only Cooper knows right now," Miles responds, making me wonder why he hasn't told anyone else. "That's why we're here and not the clubhouse. You mind skipping the meeting to stay with her later today?" he asks Eddie.

"No problem. I ain't been riding much anymore. Suspect I'll be turning in my patch soon," Eddie says sadly.

"Sorry to hear that," Miles tells him.

"Ah, can't nobody outrun time on a Harley unless you fuck up and freeze it," he replies. "This your dog?" he asks, reaching over to rub Blackjack's head. "Cute thing. What kind is it?"

"He's a mutt some kid was getting rid of out at the supermarket. Looks like he has some lab in him."

"Yeah, he does. Sparky will be happy to have a friend over," Eddie says.

"Sparky is Eddie's old bulldog," Miles explains to me. "Come on, let's get some sleep while he destroys the SUV."

"Thank God," I mutter, trying to keep the surprise off my face when Miles takes my free hand in his. I wouldn't ever expect him to be the hand holding type, but I really like it.

CHAPTER TWENTY-FIVE

Miles

I'M up and out of Eddie's guest bed as soon as the alarm on my phone goes off.

Time for the Kings' meeting.

"What?" Kira lifts her head from her pillow and asks groggily through heavy-lidded eyes.

"Go back to sleep. I've got to head out for a little while. You'll be okay here."

"Okay," she replies before her head is down again and she's out like a light.

I stagger around while I try to pull on my boots. Once my cut is in place, I'm ready to go.

Sparky's old ass gets up just to bark at me when I step out the front door, making me feel like shit. At least Jack is happy to see me with his tail wagging.

"The mutt behaving?" I ask Eddie whose head is under the hood of a truck engine a few feet away.

"Yeah. Sparky likes the company," he says.

"Good," I reply. "You got a bike I can maybe borrow?"

"Sure. Take your pick. Keys are hanging up by the door in the garage in order of my rides," he says without looking up from his project.

"Thanks," I tell him. "Any problem with the SUV?"

"Only that it smelled of death," he mutters, then finally glances over at me. "I crushed it, and whatever is left is burning now."

After he mentions it, I can smell the scent of melted plastic and oil in the air.

"I appreciate your help, Eddie."

"No problem. Tell the guys I'm babysitting, or I would be there."

"I will," I agree when I check my phone to see the time. "Actually, I need to run an errand and come back by before I go. Keep a close eye on her," I say. "But not too close."

"Yeah, yeah. I know," he chuckles.

I grab the first set of keys in Eddie's garage that go to an early model Electraglide. It easily cranks and sounds good, which is all I care about at the moment.

A quick drive later and I'm in the local pharmacy, trying to decide between a dozen different types of pregnancy tests.

I finally decide to go with the one that has several in the package, that way we won't have any doubt.

When I place the box on the counter, the young, female cashier raises her eyebrows at my purchase.

"What?" I ask her. "I'm married," I say, holding up my ring finger. "They're for my wife."

She's smart enough not to make any comments while bagging the tests before I hand over the cash and get the hell out of there.

I simply nod at Eddie when I pull back up in front of his place, then head inside to leave the bag on my empty spot in the bed for Kira to find if she wakes up before I get back.

Depending on how shit goes down after I tell the guys about the Russian shitstorm I stirred up, our meeting could take a while. Which sucks because I'm still tired as fuck and worried about Kira.

I wish we were still home in my bed naked and not dealing with a bunch of dead bastards. Hopefully soon we can get back there.

I'm one of the last to take my seat at the Savage King's table for our meeting. "Eddie's tied up," I tell Torin, so they won't keep waiting for him.

"He's going to retire soon, isn't he?" Chase asks.

"Probably. Said he's getting too old to ride."

"Well, we'll keep his seat open until he decides," Torin replies just as Reece comes in with two pink boxes and places them on the table.

"What's this?" Abe asks while reaching over to lift the lid. "Titties! My favorite," he exclaims, making the rest of us laugh when he crams two round pastries into his mouth at the same time.

"Compliments of Cynthia," Reece says as he takes his seat. "Eat them up and go buy more."

"Don't any of you tell the old ladies we devoured Cynthia's boobs today. They would never believe the truth," Abe announces with a chuckle as he licks the center.

"Let's get started so we can all get out of here," Torin says before he gets things rolling. Apparently, we've had a damn good year and payouts are coming soon.

"Let's try to keep things running smooth this year, with as few distractions as possible," Torin adds, to which everyone agrees. "That's it for me today. Mostly I just wanted to check in with everyone since most of us have our families keeping us busy lately. It's good to see you're all still in one piece," he jokes with a grin. "Now, is there any business we need to address?"

"I have something," Reece holds up his fist and says to get everyone's attention right before I give a wave of my hand.

"Me too," I tell them.

Reece seems thrilled that Cynthia is moving in to the clubhouse, which everyone gladly approves, and he's training up the prospect to help out with the security.

I'm guessing we need it since he didn't give me any shit about bringing a woman to Eddie's this morning, so he wasn't paying very close attention to the cameras.

"We ready to adjourn?" Chase asks impatiently, already sliding his chair backward.

Torin's even about to slam the gavel down when I cringe but speak up before they all disappear. "There's something I need to bring to the table."

"Oh, right. Sorry," Torin apologizes, laying the gavel back down. "Is there a problem?"

Shit. How the hell do I tell them this?

Reaching up to scratch the side of my head as I figure out the best way to explain this, I say, "Could be, yeah. Now, it's not my fault or anything, but I may have made the club a new...enemy."

"Enemy?" Reece snaps angrily at me. "What the fuck did you do, man?"

"All I was doing was protecting what's mine, same as *any* of you would've done," I respond defensively.

"What the hell happened?" Torin huffs, leaning back in his chair with his arms crossed over his chest.

"Well, I, ah, accidentally killed a fucker who may be the right-hand man to the Russian mafia boss."

Curses erupt from every mouth in the room.

"Are you serious? How did you 'accidentally' kill him?" Sax asks me.

"I put a bullet through his head," I answer honestly before adding "along with three of his buddies."

"Jesus fuck! Why the hell did you do that, man?" Cooper grumbles before the rest of them can recover enough to ask.

"Because they broke in my house to rob me or kill me, probably both," I explain. "And they were the same assholes who had been threatening my in-laws."

"I don't know which is the most confusing part of all the shit you just said, the house part or the in-laws," Reece mutters. "It definitely isn't the murdering part. That seems par for the course, so why don't you just back the fuck up and tell us what's going on, *brother*."

Reaching up to rub the back of my reddening neck because everyone is pissed at me, I tell them, "Well, I ah, bought a place out near the cape, needs a little fixing up but I got a good price."

"Oh-kay," Chase drawls. "You moved out of the clubhouse. Fine. What's with the in-laws? You're not married."

"Actually, I am," I reply, flashing them my wedding band.

"To whom?" Reece ask. "You were just trying to get with Cynthia a few months ago!"

"It's all pretty new. Things happened fast," I say in a rush since this is what I wanted to avoid, them finding out I bought Kira to be my wife. Getting to the point, I tell them, "Look, it doesn't matter. The point is, if the Russian boss knows about my ties to the MC, he could come after us when his men don't turn up."

"That's just fucking great!" War shouts at me. "Can't have a year of peace without one of you going and stirring some shit up!"

"It's not like I went looking for trouble!" I yell back at him. "I was trying to mind my own business at home when those fools broke in!"

"You were home with your...wife?" Torin asks still sounding perplexed about how I was able to convince a woman to marry me.

"Yes. My *wife*," I grit out. "We made it official six weeks ago. Coop was there."

All of their heads turn to the end of the table where Cooper silently nods his involvement before they look around at each other.

"Why hasn't anyone but Coop met her yet?" Chase asks me.

Scratching at the side of my head again to try and figure out a way to explain it without a full admission I say, "Ah, well, she's sort of shy," which causes Coop to choke out what sounds like a laugh and a cough.

"*Shy?*" Gabe who rarely talks in a meeting speaks up and says,

145

the one word heavy with skepticism. "You and *shy* don't exactly go together, bro."

"Tell me about it," I huff with a grin because the last few weeks trying to get Kira back into my bed has felt like a lifetime. "But I think I'm finally wearing her down."

"By *murdering* men?" Torin asks.

"Yeah, men who were taking every penny from her parents. Now they're done."

"Done?" Reece asks. "You're not that stupid, are you? The first names on that Russian boss's shit list is going to be her folks. You need to get them someplace safe with new names and shit, the sooner the better before he realizes his men are missing."

"Fuck," I grumble since I hadn't thought of that. I was too busy disposing of the bodies to think about her folks. "Guess you're right."

"Wow," Torin says as he scrubs both hands over his face. "The Russian mafia?"

"I didn't know it at the time," I tell him. "If I had, I wouldn't have gone straight to ending them."

Maybe.

"Well, what's done is done," Torin responds. "I'll talk to Jade and Knox. They're close friends with the east coast's Italian and Irish mafia boss."

"Holy shit! Your sister knows *both* mob bosses?" Maddox asks with awe. "She's a badass."

Torin holds up a single finger. "Jade and Knox know *the* Italian and Irish mob boss singular. Ivan killed his father, the Italian boss, and then married the daughter of the head of the Irish mafia after her father went to prison. He's been in charge of both syndicates for years and you barely hear a peep out of them now."

"Wow," Maddox responds. "Must be one tough motherfucker."

"You think he can help with the Russian problem?" I ask hopefully.

"We can't ask him to get tangled up in our shit," Torin responds. "But maybe they'll have some suggestions for how the fuck we're supposed to proceed with the Russians without it ending in a blood-bath. If I had to guess, Ivan's probably had run-ins over the years with them."

"I'm sorry," I blurt to the guys. "I didn't mean for this shit to happen. But she's my wife. What else was I supposed to do when they barge in our house?"

"Are we done for today?" Reece asks while glancing down at his watch. "Until Torin talks to Jade and Miles gets his in-laws some-where safe?"

"Yeah, I guess so," Torin agrees. "We'll meet back here in the morning to see where we're at. And we'll need you to beef up secu-rity everywhere."

"No shit," Reece mutters.

"Adjourned," Torin says with a slam of his gavel on the table. Turning to me as most of the guys jump up out of their seats, he asks, "Where's your wife now?"

"She's at the salvage yard with Eddie. That's why he stayed back," I explain.

"Good, that's good," he agrees. "I'm gonna make some calls to Jade, see if she can get us on a conference call with Ivan. You want to stick around here and see what he says?"

"Yeah, I can do that," I reply even though I would rather be in bed with Kira. Getting up from my chair, I tell him, "I'll make a few calls and be around so give me a ring when you have some information."

"Will do," Torin responds with a heavy sigh.

CHAPTER TWENTY-SIX

Kira

THE SOUND of my ringing phone pulls me out of a deep sleep. When I sit up and open my eyes, it takes several long seconds for me to remember why I'm not on the black leather sofa in our living room.

Miles killed Zeno and three other guys yesterday, so now we're hiding out at a junk yard.

Right.

The phone stops and then starts again, so I throw off the covers and scurry to pull the device from my purse.

"Hello?" I answer.

"Hey, you had me worried there for a minute," Miles says.

"Sorry, I was sleeping so good."

"I hate to wake you up, but you didn't say what your parents are going to do. Are they still at home?"

"No, my mom said they were leaving yesterday," I reply. "Why?"

"Good. That's good," Miles says with an exhale of what I think is relief. "They need to lay low someplace with no paper trail. Tell them to use cash, no credit cards for all purchases and not to use their real names if they stay at a hotel."

"Okay. I'll call them now," I assure him, thinking it's sweet that he's worried about my parents. "Are you on your way back?"

"No, not yet," he grumbles. "I have to stay around here for a while, but I promise I'll be back as soon as I can."

"Yeah, sure, that's fine."

"There are some tests in the bag I left on the bed," he tells me, and I glance over to see for myself.

"Should I wait, or do you want me to go ahead?"

"Up to you," Miles says. "I thought you might want to get it over with, find out for sure."

"Yeah, I do," I agree. "But I want to wait until you're here too."

"We can do that, whatever you decide," Miles says. "Just hang tight and I'll see you soon."

"Okay, bye," I say before he ends the call.

Concerned about my parents' safety, I call my mother's cell phone next. She quickly tells me that they are fine and actually enjoying themselves on vacation in Florida, so I withhold from them the fact that Zeno and the others are dead. They took out cash from the bank before they left so there's no way for Kozlov to track them down. Eventually their money will run out, though. I'm not sure what will happen then...

For now, all I know is that my mouth is so dry that I need about a gallon of water, so I slip into the kitchen. I'm looking for a glass when Eddie says, "I thought I heard you up and moving around."

"I'm so thirsty I could drink out of the sink. You mind if I..."

"Help yourself," he says with a wave of his hand. "Get any sleep?"

"I did, thanks."

"Blackjack must have had a rough night too. He's curled up asleep with Sparky," he tells me with a grin.

"Aww. I'm glad they're getting along."

"Me too," Eddie agrees. "How about I clean up and fix us some lunch?"

"You don't have to go to any trouble," I tell him.

"How about an omelet since we missed breakfast?"

"That would be great," I say when my palm goes to my growling stomach. I especially need the sustenance if I'm eating for two.

After I get cleaned up in the bathroom, Eddie tells me to sit at the bar when I offer to help. I don't miss the fact that there's a gun-shaped lump under the back of his shirt or that, even while he cooks, he keeps an eye out the kitchen window.

"There you go," he says when he slides a plate in front of me and then cuts into his own omelet with a fork while standing at the bar.

I take a bite, and tell him, "This is delicious, Eddie."

"Glad you like it," he says between bites. "You must be important to Miles. I've never seen him care enough to be protective of a woman before."

"He's good to me," I say.

"Is he?" he asks, not sarcastically but like he's curious.

"Yeah, he is."

"Honestly, I wasn't sure, especially with the dishonorable discharge. Then the court martial prison sentence," Eddie tells me. "Miles keeps to himself most of the time, and I don't blame him. Men don't usually come back from war or prison the way they go in. I didn't know him before, but I'm guessing he's a different man now and struggles with it each day."

Miles was kicked out of the military and went to prison? Wow. I wonder why.

"He told me he was in the Marines," I say. "Is that where he got his tattoos?"

"Maybe."

"You don't know what they mean?" I ask.

"Even if I did, he'll need to tell you his own ghost stories."

"Ghost stories?" I ask with my fork frozen in the air.

151

"Did Miles tell you what he did in the Marines?" Eddie asks.

"He said he was a sniper, that he's good with guns," I reply.

"And what exactly is it you think Marine snipers do with their guns during wars?"

"Oh," I mutter in understanding. "He killed people."

"They don't shoot to injure," he responds.

"But he's a good man even if he kills people."

"Anything is possible," Eddie tells me. "And as long as he's good to you, does it really matter?"

When a phone starts buzzing, I jump up from my stool, thinking it's mine, but then Eddie's fork clatters to his plate as he pulls out his and reads the screen.

"Shit," he grumbles.

"Everything okay?" I ask.

"Yeah, but I have a feeling Miles is going to have some MC business keeping him busy for a while."

I don't think much of that statement until he goes to the front door and holds it open, whistling for Sparky, who slowly waddles in with Blackjack on his heels, happily bouncing around with his new friend. When I go over to scoop up Jack, Eddie shuts the door and then turns about three different locks on it, making me nervous.

"Just locking the place down as a precaution," he says when he starts to the back door.

"Are you sure Miles is okay?" I ask him in concern.

"Oh, yeah, doll. He'll be just fine."

The racing heart in my chest, however, doesn't believe him.

Miles

AFTER TORIN MAKES a call to Jade, and we wait, I need to keep moving, do something.

"I'm going to see if Gabe can give me some ink while we wait for them to call back," I tell Torin.

"Yeah, I'll let you know when we set the call up."

With a nod, I head up the stairs and out of the bar, crossing the street to the tattoo studio.

When I walk inside, a jingle sounds, causing Gabe to glance up from his desk in the corner.

"What's up?" he asks when he stands and comes over to me.

"You got time to ink me?"

"Sure," he responds. "I've got the black ready to go, figured you would want to add four more birds."

"That and some lettering here," I tell him, pointing to the inside of my forearm.

"Cursive freehand work?" he asks.

"Yeah, I trust you," I reply. The kid's got a steady hand and is a genius with a needle.

"Let's get started then," Gabe says. "Have a seat in the first chair and I'll go wash up."

"Thanks," I tell him as he disappears into the back.

When he returns, I've removed my shirt and cut, and Gabe's gloved up and ready to get to work.

"You want the new four here?" he asks, rubbing his fingertip over the upper part of my ribs.

"Yep."

"Got it," he says before he starts cleaning the area.

"You talked to Ian lately?" I ask him to fill the silence and because I haven't heard much from our brother lately.

"Been a few weeks. Why?" he asks tersely.

"Just wondering how he was doing."

"He's getting through," Gabe replies. "Crankier every time I see him."

"No shit," I mutter. I spent plenty of years behind bars myself, so I hate it for him. "When's his release date?"

"Ah, I think he's got about another year left if he doesn't fuck it up and get any more violations. I can't believe he got hit with some fucked-up assault charge and ruined his good behavior days."

"Still a year, really?" I ask. "Seems like he's been in that fucking place forever."

"Four years, ten months and eleven days," Gabe says off the top of his head. "Not that I'm keeping count or anything."

"Right," I drawl over the sound of the buzzing needle. "You were still a prospect when he went in, weren't you?"

"Yeah."

"Still can't believe he was stupid enough to speed while carrying."

"Me either," Gabe grumbles. "One fucking mistake cost him five years of his life, and he blames me for it."

"You? Why would he blame you?" I ask in confusion.

"No clue," he quickly responds before clearing his throat and saying, "Birds are done and small enough you won't need any wrapping on them. You want to write out the lettering or tell it to me so I can figure out the spacing?"

"Ah, yeah," I agree as he wipes the area on my ribs clean and I pull my shirt back down to sit up in the chair.

"Let me grab some paper and a pen," Gabe says before he gets up and then returns with a notepad in his gloved hands. "Ready when you are."

"Okay," I say. "I will share my life with you, build our dreams together, support you through times of trouble and rejoice with you in times of happiness. I promise to give you respect, love and loyalty through all the trials and triumphs of our lives together."

When Gabe doesn't say anything, I look over and tell him, "That's it. That's all of it."

"Wow, man," he replies as he blinks his long, dark eyelashes rapidly.

"Are you fucking crying?" I huff.

"No. No, absolutely not."

"Yeah, you are. You can't fucking tattoo me when you're crying!"

"Give me a second," he says before he puts the notebook down on the side table and wanders off into the back.

When he comes back, I ask him, "Did you find your balls?"

"I'm a sensitive guy, and it's sweet," he mutters. "Especially for a tough guy like you."

"Yeah, well, it's not like I came up with it or anything. It was our wedding vows," I explain. "I just memorized them."

"You love her," Gabe replies with a grin.

"What? It's not like that," I disagree. "You know the things I've done. I'm a cold, heartless murderer. You've seen the birds and added to them. You know how many kills I have."

"So?" he asks.

"So, how could I ever really love someone?"

"Do you want her to be happy?" Gabe asks.

"Yes."

"And you worry about her?"

"All the fucking time," I grumble.

"You would do anything to protect her?" he asks as if that's even a question.

"Damn right I would."

"Then you love her, man."

"That's it?" I ask. "That's love?"

"That's love. And you don't just love her, but you love your brothers too," he suggests.

"Fine, I guess I do love her," I cave and agree. "But how could she ever possibly love me, though?"

"Same way all the Kings love you, for all the reasons I just listed," Gabe says.

"Yeah, but you all know who I *really* am, that I'm a killer. She doesn't."

"Does she know about the Russians you killed?"

155

"Yes." Chuckling, I tell him, "She helped me get rid of them last night."

"Then she knows you, man! She's your ride or die girl who knows you, and she's sticking around," he responds, then pauses. "Hold on. You aren't *making* her stick around, are you?"

"No. I told her she could leave, and she said she wanted to stay." *At least for now.* While Kira may know about the Russians, she doesn't know about all of my kills. If she did, she would go running the other way.

"Then there you go!" Gabe exclaims. "Mystery solved. You love each other. Why would you get married if you didn't?"

"I think she's pregnant," I tell him, ignoring his question about how we came to be married and glad to share the news with someone.

"No shit? And it's your kid?"

"Yeah, it's mine."

"Then congratulations! That's amazing news. Why didn't you tell the guys at the table today?" he asks.

"We don't know for sure yet," I reply. "But she's late and I fucked her, so, yeah, she's probably knocked up. Right?"

"Ah, yeah, sounds like it," Gabe says with a grin. "You should tell the others. They'll be happy for you and may not be as pissed off at you for the Russian mafia mess since you were protecting your family."

"You think so?" I ask.

"Definitely," he agrees. "Now give me your arm and let's ink those vows for your woman to see. She's going to fucking love it."

"I hope so," I tell him.

Gabe is on the word triumph in the second sentence when both of our phones start buzzing simultaneously, so it must be a Kings' alert going out to everyone.

"Not yet. Almost finished," Gabe says, holding my arm still.

A few minutes later and he's done. As soon as the needle is off my skin, I'm digging my phone out of my jean pocket, figuring it's something from Torin about the conference call.

"Fuck," I grumble as I read the text message. "Cynthia's missing, and Reece thinks her ex has her."

"Fuck," Gabe agrees as he pulls off his gloves and gets to his feet.

"Sax said we all need to hit the road and look for a nineties model, blue Dodge truck with a black scuff on the passenger side."

"Let's ride," Gabe says.

CHAPTER TWENTY-SEVEN

Miles

I'VE BEEN on the road for over an hour looking for the blue truck when I feel my phone buzzing inside my cut pocket. As soon as I can pull over on the shoulder, I look to see what it says.

Cynthia was found and is at the hospital.

Thank fuck.

I know Reece was going out of his mind and went ballistic when Torin told him to stay at the clubhouse and wait for a call. Our president was right. He had no business on the road until she was found. I bet he broke every traffic law in the state to get to the hospital. Hopefully she's in good shape.

I turn my bike around and head back to the clubhouse to get details. Sax pulls up when I do, and it looks like we're the last to make it back.

"You heard how she's doing?" he asks.

"No."

"After we found the blood in her apartment, I'm guessing it's not good," he mutters as we start down the basement steps, then join the rest of the guys in the chapel, minus Reece.

"Any updates?" Sax asks when he takes his seat and I go around the table to pull out my chair.

"Jade said Cynthia's in bad shape. Vicky too, but they think they're both gonna make it."

Everyone lets out a simultaneous sigh of relief.

"I just had to go and say things have been quiet," Torin grumbles while rubbing his temple like he's got a killer headache. "It is good to have everyone back in, except for Reece. We should be getting a call from Ivan soon about the Russians. I'll put it on speaker so we can all hear."

Fuck. As if we need to deal with my shit when Reece is going through hell.

We all sit in silence, lost in our own thoughts until his phone starts ringing.

"Torin," our president answers. "Thanks for getting back to us so soon, Ivan. Mind if I put you on speaker for my guys to hear?"

Ivan must approve, because Torin removes the phone from his ear and hits the speaker button before placing the device near the center of the table.

"So, have you had any dealings with the Russians?" Torin asks.

"I've talked to the boss a few times," a young guy's voice tells us. "His name is Boris Kozlov. His supply comes in through imports, usually hidden within legit crates to get through customs. He has guys here in Greensboro who keep his pipeline moving, and they're not big fans of the Italians or Irish."

"What do they import?" Chase asks.

"Heroin and big guns from what I've heard. They have guys up and down the coast bringing the shit in and distributing it."

"I guess Jade told you about our situation. Any advice for how to handle killing Kozlov's men?"

"I talked to my people in Charleston. That's the Russian's biggest port because it's smaller, fewer eyes on it, less red tape," Ivan says. "Zeno is the guy who handles US distribution, and he's next in line to take over."

"Was," I speak up and say. "He was next in line, but now he's dead."

"Then I expect you have a huge problem on your hands," Ivan tells us. "Zeno isn't just high up in their hierarchy. He's also Kozlov's cousin."

"Fucking hell," everyone curses in some shape or form.

"He'll notice he's missing soon, if he hasn't already. They stay in touch on a daily basis. Is there any trail that will lead them to the Kings?" Ivan asks.

"Yes," I reluctantly answer. "My wife's family gave up my name after he beat her father. That's why Zeno paid us a visit. We assume he wanted money, but I never took the time to ask him."

"In that case, you can safely assume that Kozlov knows who you are too. I'm betting Zeno called to tell him as soon as he got the information," Ivan suggests.

"That's just fucking great," War huffs.

"So, we should be ready for an attack?" Torin asks Ivan through clenched teeth.

"Kozlov has men in every state up and down the east coast. It won't take them long to get to you."

"Sax, go find a safe house for the women and children," our president orders. "As soon as there's someplace that will hold them all, set it up and put out the notice that the women should pack and go immediately."

"On it," Sax says before he gets up and leaves the room.

"Instead of waiting for the Russians to come to you, what if you ambush them first?" Ivan suggests.

"How exactly would we do that?" Torin asks.

"Easy," Ivan tells him. "I invite Kozlov for a sit-down in Greensboro. A party of sorts. He'll come and bring his top guys, all but a few on the coast who will be looking for the Kings. They'll never know what hit them."

"You think you can make that happen and fast?" Torin asks.

"I'll tell him I'm ready to get back in the heroin trade and I want him to be my supplier. He's greedy enough to take me up on it. He knows he's getting two syndicates' orders for the price of one with me."

"If you can get him here this week, it could work," Torin agrees.

"I'm confident he'll bite. It wouldn't be unusual for me to ask him how many men he's expecting so that I can provide them with complementary accommodations."

"That's perfect," Chase says with a grin. "Then we can triple his numbers."

"I can't make my men help you, but I can ask for volunteers for the event. There are always a few who love to blow off some steam with a bloodbath. They haven't had a chance in a long time."

"We understand and can't ask you to risk yourself or your men," Torin tells him. "We can get a group together, so no pressure."

"You're doing me a favor. If you take out all the Russians, then the entire east coast is mine."

"How fucking old are you?" Maddox speaks up and asks.

"Just turned twenty-two. Why?" Ivan answers.

"How do you run two mafias when you can barely drink?" the kid questions him, making us all scowl in his direction.

"Because I've got a big dick and brass balls," he responds, making us chuckle.

"Sorry, Ivan," Torin says while glaring at Maddox. "You have to ignore our newest member. He's your age and in awe of your bad-ass-ness."

"No problem," Ivan responds, not sounding bothered by the ridiculous question. "So, I'll check in with Kozlov and get back to you if he agrees."

"Thanks, man, we really appreciate your help," Torin tells him right before the call ends. "Did you really have to ask him that?" he questions Maddox.

"Sorry. It's just...he's so young!"

"A leader makes good decisions," Torin replies. "Not many young guys have the experience to think through shit all the way around, but who knows, maybe you'll be President of the Kings before you're thirty."

Jaws drop at that statement.

"You planning on going somewhere?" Chase asks his brother in concern.

"No. But a change in leadership is good every once in a while. In a few years, I may want to hand over the gavel to let someone else deal with all your fuckups."

"Sorry," I say again.

"We're going to handle this," Torin says. "First, we get the women and kids the hell out of town. Then we'll come up with a plan for if and when Ivan gets Kozlov to the states. If you killed his cousin, then I'm betting he's already booked his plane ticket, so Ivan's invitation will be nothing more than a pitstop."

"Guess we'll see soon enough."

"What about retaliation?" War asks. "If we don't get them all..."

"I know," Torin agrees. "We can't eliminate the Russian mafia entirely, but only an idiot would try to fight back against the Irish, Italians and Kings when they have the kind of casualties we're about to hand them."

"I hope you're right," War mutters just as Sax comes back and retakes his seat.

"For now, let's check on our brother, see if Reece needs anything before we send the ladies packing," Torin says. "I want someone to stay behind with Reece in case the Russians come to town while we're gone. His head isn't in the right place to have to watch his back too while Cynthia's in the hospital. Any volunteers?"

"Gabriel can stay," Abe speaks up and says, volunteering his brother, who flips him off from across the table.

"You don't get to assign me to babysitting duty when you're going into the line of fire too, bro," Gabe responds.

"I'll stay," Coop volunteers.

"Good."

"I just talked to the Myrtle Beach charter," Sax says. "They can house our family members in one of their beachfront houses in Surfside. They rent it out through a real estate company so no one would think to find them there."

"Sounds like a great plan," Torin agrees. "I want the girls to stay together and Cedric to keep watch with the MB Kings."

"Don't we need Cedric on security while Reece is at the hospital?" Chase asks.

"Shit," Torin mutters. "You're right. We need Cedric and Eddie watching the security cameras *remotely*, not on site here at the Asylum. It's too dangerous."

"Peyton will have her gun on her," Dalton announces.

"Lexi will be armed too," Torin replies. "Guess we'll have to make do and trust the MB Kings to protect them."

"They will," War grumbles. "Or they'll be our next stop."

"Are we closing shop?" Gabe asks.

"I want everything shut down until further notice," Torin agrees. "Your shop, The Jolly Roger, Avalon, the Asylum. None of us will be around to run them anyway."

"Right," Gabe agrees.

"Cooper, don't let Reece out of your sight," Torin orders. "Help him however you can while he's hurting."

"Got it," Coop agrees. "I'll head to the hospital now."

"And I'll get the message sent to the women and to the other charters to let them know we're going to war," Sax announces.

"Maybe we should get some of the Virginia crew down here to hang around town," Abe suggests.

"Fine, but I don't want anyone wearing a cut until this mess is over," Torin says. "No reason to put a giant target on our backs."

Damn, you know shit is at rock bottom for the Kings when our pres tells us to take off the cuts.

Hopefully this mess will all be over soon, and things can get back to normal.

They have to, because my life was finally getting good with my wife.

I love Kira. And I've waited too long for some thugs to end this for me now.

CHAPTER TWENTY-EIGHT

Kira

MILES HAS BEEN GONE for hours. All I've been doing is sitting here worrying, wondering if he's okay. Eddie has been on high alert, constantly checking outside. Even Sparky has been jumpy, barking at every sound he hears.

After the third hour, I caved and took all three of the pregnancy tests. I needed something to keep me busy while I waited for Miles to call or get back here.

Finally, just as the sun is about to set, I hear the rumbling of a motorcycle.

Eddie is up out of his chair and looking out the blinds before I can even register the sound. "It's him," he says.

"Thank god," I say on an exhale.

When I pick up Blackjack and go to unlock the door, Eddie stops me by putting his arm in front of the locks.

"I can't let you go out there."

"Why not?" I turn and ask him indignantly.

"It's not safe."

"But Miles is out there."

"Yeah, and he has a gun on him. He'll be on the porch in a second; and when he is, I'll unlock the door."

"Fine," I say when I give up and take a step back to wait.

A moment later and Eddie starts unlocking each deadbolt before pulling it open.

Moving so fast he's a leather and jean blur, Miles is wrapping his arms around me and Jack.

"I was worried about you," I tell him when he crushes me to him.

"I was worried about you too," he says when he pulls away. "You mind taking Blackjack for a long walk?" Miles asks Eddie as he takes the dog from my arms. After giving Jack a scratch behind his ears, he hands him over to the older man.

"Just call when you want me to come back in," Eddie says with a chuckle on the way to the door.

"I thought it wasn't safe," I remind him.

"I have a gun too," Eddie remarks before he leaves.

"What's going on?" I ask Miles.

Both of his hands grab either side of my shirt and lift it over my head. His mouth comes down on the top of my breasts heaving from the cups of my bra while his fingers work on undoing my pants.

"What's going on is I'm getting you naked and then fucking you over the back of this sofa."

"Oh," I say in a breathless gasp when Miles hits his knees to drag my jeans and panties down my legs. As soon as my shoes and socks are off, and my legs are bare, Miles buries his face between my legs.

"I missed breakfast and lunch, so I have to eat your pussy before and after I fuck you," he says before his tongue swipes through my slit, parting my flesh and getting it nice and wet for his big cock. As if I'm not slick enough to take him already after hearing him say he was going to bend me over and fuck me.

Once I'm soaking wet, he finally rubs the tip of his tongue over the place I'm desperate for it.

"God, yes!" I scream as he attacks my clit and slips a finger deep inside of me at the same time.

Miles is a master at oral. He has me coming on his tongue faster than a speeding bullet. So much faster than I ever came using my little vibrating bullet.

"Yes, yes, yes!" I chant as my fingers tug on his hair holding his face against my body while jolts of red-hot pleasure rack my entire body.

My eyes are still closed, soaking in the bliss when Miles is up and pressing his hand to my upper back, guiding me down over the back of the sofa.

I hear his zipper being pulled down, and then he's rubbing his swollen cockhead back and forth through my soaked pussy lips.

"Please," I tell him as I press back and lift my bottom, needing to feel him inside of me.

Miles feeds his cock into my pussy one slow inch at a time. When he's fully seated and it's impossible for me to take anymore, he leans over my back, reaches around to jerk the cups of my bra down and then palms my breasts in each hand.

My inner walls clench around him, still spasming from the amazing orgasm.

"Fuck me, Miles," I tell him as I squirm underneath him.

"You have no idea how much I love hearing those words come out of your mouth," he says, placing a soft kiss on the side of my cheek before he pulls his hips back, nearly taking all his cock away from me before slamming in so hard I cry out.

"More, please," I gasp as my fingers grip the sofa, trying to hold on when he finally can't contain himself any longer.

I don't know what I enjoy more, his grunts and groans above me or the amazing way he feels inside of me in this position.

Miles was the first man to fuck me from behind, and it's so good when he's rubbing me at this angle that I'm not sure why anyone would have sex any other way.

"This pussy was made for me, princess," Miles says before he bites down on my shoulder between brutal thrusts. "I can't get enough."

"Take it," I tell him. "It's yours. I'm yours."

"Damn right you are," he agrees. Letting go of my breasts, Miles leans back and then slaps my ass cheek. "Work that ass on your cock. Show me how bad you want it now that it's all yours."

"I want it so bad," I tell him as I swivel my hips and push back to force his shaft deeper.

"You need my hand right here too, don't you?" he asks when his palm reaches around and grabs my pussy possessively. "I know exactly how to get my wife off. You need my hard cock and a little clit tickle, princess?"

"God yes, I love it," I say when his magical fingers send me soaring while he fucks my brains out. He thrusts so deep and hard that my teeth chatter and I almost bite my tongue. I still want more when it's all over and his cock slips free leaving me slumped over the sofa, unable to move a muscle.

But apparently Miles isn't done blowing my mind just yet. I realize he wasn't lying about eating me afterward when his tongue snakes up the inside of my thigh, licking up the mess we made.

"You don't have to –" I start to say before he French kisses my clit, sucking it, licking it, and turning my brains to mush.

"Don't stop, don't stop," I chant over and over in time with my bouncing hips that are racing toward another release.

God, he's so good to me. I'm not sure what I did to deserve such an amazing man who takes care of me in every possible way, but I'll never get enough.

"*Ahh!*" I shout when I plummet over the crest and down yet again with the end nowhere in sight. It's the longest, most intense orgasm I've ever had; and by the time my body stops shaking, I can't hold myself up any longer.

Miles sweeps me off my feet and into his arms, causing the world to spin. The door to the bedroom shuts. Then, he lowers me to the guest bed and stretches out alongside me so that we're face to face.

"Thank you," I tell him, grabbing his jaw with one weak hand and pulling his lips to my mouth, loving how my flavor mixes with his.

CHAPTER TWENTY-NINE

Miles

"You have to leave," I whisper against Kira's lips while I hold her to me, trying to soak up as much of her warm, tantalizing scent as possible before I have to let her go.

"What?" she asks, reeling back while the hazy lust fades from her eyes.

"We're making plans to ambush the Russians, hopefully before they show up here," I explain. "All the women and kids are going to stay down in Surfside Beach with the Myrtle Beach Savage Kings charter until it's safe. I don't want you to go, but it's the best thing to make sure you are out of the crossfire if any of them come to town before we pull off our trap."

"Okay. When do I have to go?" she asks.

"Soon," I reply. "Chase said you could get a ride with Sasha and Mercy. They'll call when they're on the way."

"What about Blackjack?"

"I'm sure Eddie will stick around. He can take care of him until you get back."

"I'll miss him," she says.

"I know."

"I'll miss you too," she adds, slipping her palm up the bottom of my shirt and placing it on my side, right on top of the new ink. "Why don't you ever get undressed when we're together?" Kira asks.

"Because I'm not sure if you're ready to see all of the darkness inside of me," I reply honestly.

"I've seen most of you," she says. "You were shirtless when you were mowing the yard. I want to see all of your tattoos."

"What if you can't handle it and run?"

"I'm not running," Kira assures me as she pushes my cut down my shoulders. "I just want to see, touch, and kiss every inch of my husband. It's not fair for you to look like you do and keep your body hidden from me."

I've never hesitated to show a woman before or tell her about the tally I keep inked on my side, but Kira is different. I care what she thinks about me, and I don't want to lose her when she sees how many lives I've taken.

Then I catch the fresh ink on my forearm from the corner of my eye.

The first sentence is, *"I will share my life with you."*

Sharing my life includes the good with the bad, although most of it is bad.

Here's hoping she can take it.

I help her push my shirt up and over my head, and don't have time to catch my breath before Kira's head lowers and her lips brush my skin right below my belly button before climbing higher, heading toward the birds.

Glancing up at my face, she asks, "Will you tell me about them, your tattoos?"

God, the way she looks at me, I would give her anything she

wants. Even all of me. "The birds are how many men I've killed," I blurt out, ready to get the worst over with.

"Wow," Kira says, her eyes bulging and mouth gaping at the flock. Then...she starts counting each one with her index finger. "Forty-three?" she asks.

"Yep."

"Did they deserve it?" she asks, which is the last question I was expecting. I figured she would be appalled, ask me what's wrong in my sick fucking head that could cause me to take forty-three lives, and if I have any remorse.

I don't.

Except for one.

"Why is this one red?" she questions, pointing to the one in the middle before I can respond to her last question.

"Because he's the only one I didn't enjoy killing," I tell her. "And the only one who didn't deserve to die."

"Oh?" she says, and it sounds like a question.

"Ryan Foster was my spotter, the guy who watched my back, called targets, and helped me line up my shots. He was training to be a sniper, too. We had been working as a team for months. Us against the enemy," I start to explain.

"What happened to him?"

It takes me awhile to find the words to describe the memory that I keep locked up inside of me, one I wish I could forget. I've never told any of my MC brothers what happened, why I went to prison. But I want to tell Kira, to finally get it off my chest. Then she'll know all of my demons and can decide if she can handle them.

"Our squad was part of an operation to run the Taliban out of a village in Afghanistan," I start. "Ryan and I were in position on the side of a mountain, up above the tree line, where we could get a clear line-of-sight. Our job was to pick off high priority targets while artillery softened the place up. Anyhow," I take a deep breath to brace myself for the hollow ache that always forms in my chest when I think about that day.

"After I picked off a couple of guys, Ryan spotted one dude giving orders and moving some mortars into position to start throwing shells our way. I told him not to worry. Those goat farmers always fired at the trees; they had no idea how we operated. I never fired from that kind of cover."

"Why not?" Kira interrupts. "Isn't it safer than just being out in the open on the mountain?"

"Huh? Oh, hell no," I reply. "They couldn't see us, so they were just firing blindly. If you're out in the open, the chances of them hitting you are almost zilch. If you're in the woods, though, they're going to be blowing up trunks, limbs, knocking shit over on top of you. Taking mortar fire in the woods is a nightmare."

"Oh," she says. "Sounds dangerous."

"It was. But we were a damn good team. Ryan helped me line up a clean shot on the officer giving the orders, and I put a bullet in his mouth while he was still shouting. About five seconds later I realized that bastard had gotten the last laugh on us. It must not have been his first rodeo, because he had his boys firing those mortars way the hell up the side of the mountain, above our position. Next thing I know, Ryan is dragging me to my feet and trying to run while half the damn mountain is sliding down around the two of us."

I notice that while I've been talking, I've wrapped Kira in a one-armed hug and squeezed her tight to my chest. I loosen my grip on her, afraid I'm choking her, but she leans into me reassuringly. "You don't have to go on, if you don't want to right now," she whispers.

"You need to know," I reply. "Living with me means living with the things I've done. Ryan was smaller than me, and that dude could move. He practically danced across that landslide, leading us to an overhang where we could get some cover. We might have made it, if there hadn't been a squad of Taliban grunts down in the trees below us. I guess they were sent out to flank our forces coming into the city; but once they spotted us moving, they opened fire. I saw the blood spray when Ryan got hit just ahead of me and grabbed him under the arms before he collapsed. I was trying to drag him into cover when this big-ass boulder came bouncing down on us and crushed his legs."

"Jesus," Kira shudders. "That's some 'Final Destination' level of horror. But how can you blame yourself for your friend dying like that?"

"Oh, that didn't kill him," I say. "That little dude was mean and tough; it was one of the reasons we got along so well together. I managed to drag him out of their line of fire, but he had been shot right above his hip," I tell her, pointing to a spot on my stomach. "The bullet had gone all the way across, right to left, just under his body armor. You could tell right away from the smell his guts were torn up. Get this, though," I snorted. "He looks over at me while the mountains coming down around us and bullets are flying by, while he's bleeding out no less, digs around in his kit for a moment, and throws me a roll of fucking duct tape. I remember just staring at it and starting to laugh, and I asked him if he really thought I was going to be able to put him back together with it."

"What did he say?" Kira prompts me gently.

"He got to laughing a little too, then told me the tape was for my leg. I didn't even notice how bad my calf was burning until he said something, but a bullet had ripped clean through me," I explain. I take her hand and place it down on my right calf, rubbing her palm across the tattoos covering the scars until she can feel the hard, puckered skin where the bullet had passed through me.

Kira grins at me. "You duct taped a bullet wound in your leg?"

"Yeah, seemed like a good idea at the time. You know I still can't grow any hair there to this day because of that damn tape? I wrapped my calf tight to close the wound, and by the time I was able to peel that shit off, my leg was smoother than yours."

"Hey, no fair, I don't have my razor with me out here!" Kira laughs. "I'm not willing to try anything as drastic as getting shot and taping myself up for permanent hair control, so I'll just have to remember to bring my toiletries when we have these 'outings' in the future."

I draw her close to me again, basking in her warmth and the smell of her hair before I continue. I haven't given anyone the full story ever since my court-martial, but I want Kira to understand exactly what happened, and hopefully judge me accordingly.

"I tried to help him," I finally manage to croak out, "but Ryan wouldn't let me. He knew he was done and wouldn't even let me see where he was shot. So instead, I laid down beside him and got my rifle ready. I was going to stay right there and hold those bastards off as long as I could. As soon as he saw what I was doing, though, he elbowed me out of the way and tried to take the rifle. He told me to get the hell out of there while he covered me."

"So you left him to save yourself?"

"Yes and no," I reply. "Ryan told me to make a break for it but said that he might black out if he moved too much. He told me to watch over him if I made it to the tree line, and if it looked like they were going to capture him...to end him. You didn't want to let the Taliban capture you, no matter what. The things they would do to American prisoners...well, that's not the point. Looking back on it, I should've thrown that stubborn son-of-a-bitch over my shoulder and just run, but at the time...my leg was on fire, and I was terrified. I wasn't thinking about anything but myself. So, I fucking did it. Ryan took my rifle, and once he had their attention, I bolted down a little ravine and made it to the trees. I hid there while they exchanged fire and saw when those grunts finally crept up the hill and drug Ryan out. He was groaning when they threw him down, so he definitely wasn't dead yet.

"What...what did you do?" Kira whispers.

"I honored his last request. I still had my pistol, and even at that range, I was able to put a round in his skull. I made sure those bastards wouldn't torture him or parade him around, and then...then I ran."

"Is that why you were dishonorably discharged?" Kira asks softly.

"How did you know that?" I question.

"Eddie."

"Oh. Yeah," I say. "I was dishonorably discharged and served five years in prison."

"You put him out of his misery. It was a horrible kindness, but it was a kindness," she says, much to my surprise.

"That's not how the Marines work. We're a team, and you never leave a man behind."

"If you had it to do all over again, would you have done anything differently?" she asks.

Releasing a heavy sigh, I tell her the truth, "No. Probably not. I wouldn't be here if I had tried to save him."

"That's nothing you should feel guilty about. If he was badly injured, even if you got him to safety, do you think he would have survived?"

"There's a chance the medic could've stopped the bleeding."

"A slim chance maybe. Not as good as the chances of you getting out of there and coming home," Kira says. "If you had died there, I wouldn't have ever met you, we wouldn't have gotten married the day we met, and," she adds, taking my hand and placing it on her stomach, "we wouldn't have created a life together."

"You took the tests?" I ask in surprise since I thought she was going to wait.

"I took the tests. All three were positive. They're in the bathroom if you want to see for yourself."

"You're really pregnant," I choke out as I cup the side of her face.

"I'm pregnant," she repeats with a grin.

"And you don't care if you married a monster and are having a kid with him? That I've taken the lives of so many men and enjoyed killing all but one?"

"You're not a monster. All humans are dangerous in the right situations. If you weren't a trained killer, Zeno would've ended us," Kira points out. Covering the hand on the side of her face with her own, she says, "I like that you can protect me, that you can stand up to anyone or anything and not back down. You did what my father couldn't do in thirty years. He was terrified of Zeno and Kozlov. He lived in constant fear because of their bullying."

"I'm sure your father did the best he could," I tell her, inwardly pleased more than words can express that she doesn't hate me for who and what I am. "He didn't have the full force of the Savage Kings MC to back him up like I do."

Trailing her fingertips down my arm, Kira says, "That's so incredibly..."

"What?" I ask.

"Hot."

"Hot?" I repeat in shock.

"Oh, yeah," she says when she throws her leg over my hip and rides me down until I'm flat on my back. She slides down my legs and then kisses my pelvis right above my waistband while her hands get to work unzipping my jeans that I left unbuttoned when I put my dick away before carrying her to bed.

Kira tugs the material down until my hardening cock pops free. Looking up at me with her eyes a million shades of blue and her lips inches away from my shaft, she asks, "What's your plan for the Russians? Are you going to try and kill Boris Kozlov?"

"Hell yes," I promise her, and my declaration of murder is rewarded with a swipe of her hot, wet tongue over the crown of my cock. "We're planning to attack his whole crew when they least expect – oh shit!" I exclaim when her lips part to take more than half my length into her mouth. "Those fuckers will...never bother your... father again," I assure her while she bobs her head up and down on my hard dick.

Unable to take any more of her teasing mouth, I grab her underneath her arms and pull her up my body so that her bare pussy is straddling my cock and her lips are on mine. She kisses me hard, her tongue forcing its way against mine. When both my palms reach around to get a handful of her amazing ass, she grabs each of my wrists; and then I let her pin them above my head on the pillow.

"This time I get to be in control," she says, smiling against my lips while her slick slit rubs along the length of my shaft and her fingers interlace with mine.

"Fuck, yes, princess. Take whatever you want from me," I tell her, giving her hands a squeeze.

"I need you inside me," Kira says urgently. With a tilt of her hips, she completely sheathes herself on me in one try. "Oh my god, yes!" she shouts, her eyes closing in bliss while her teeth bite down on her bottom lip.

My wife is the most gorgeous woman I've ever seen, and I'm so damn lucky to be inside of her.

I may have paid half a million to marry her, but it feels like I'm the one who played the lottery and won the jackpot.

CHAPTER THIRTY

Kira

"GOD, Miles, I'm gonna...come so hard," I tell him as I ride him furiously. In this position, my clit is getting rubbed in exactly the right way.

I've changed my mind. I think I like being on top, being in charge, better than doggy style.

No, I like when he's deep inside of me from behind.

Who am I kidding? How can I pick when every time I'm with Miles it just feels fucking incredible?

"Jesus, you're fucking me so good," he says from underneath me, his hands still pinned down by mine.

He's so sexy, laid out before me, finally shirtless.

The fact that he's killed so many men shouldn't have me this turned on, that I can't ride him hard and fast enough, racing to the finish line.

"Oh yeah," Miles groans while his body rolls underneath me.

"Work that pussy on your cock. It's yours, princess. That's your cock you're riding. Mount up and take it whenever you need it."

"*Yes!*" I shout when my eyes slam shut as my inner walls begin contracting around his steely girth. "Come inside what's yours so I know who I belong to."

"Oh...shit," Miles grunts as his shaft swells and his hot, thick release pulses within me.

My hips ride him frantically through the spikes of pleasure until I can barely hold myself up any longer.

As I blink my lust-heavy eyes open again, I see the shiny black words inked on the inside of Miles forearm.

Were those there before? If so, I don't remember seeing them.

It takes me a few seconds to read the beautiful cursive, flowing loops before I realize what they are, making me gasp.

Our wedding vows.

"What is it?" Miles asks. "You gonna be sick?"

"No." Then I read them aloud between sniffles, "*I will share my life with you...build our dreams together...support you through times of trouble and...rejoice with you in times of happiness. I promise to give you respect...love and loyalty...through all the trials and triumphs of our lives together.*"

"I love you," Miles says, his dark eyes locked on mine. "And I always keep my promises, but it's nice to have the reminder handy..."

"Miles," I start. That's when he finally frees his hands from mine and places his index finger to my lips. "You don't have to say it back. I know you didn't marry me to try and find love. You did it out of love for your parents. And finding out the sacrifice you made for them makes me love you even more."

"I love you too," I tell him against his finger before I bite it gently and suck on it suggestively.

"Goddamn," he groans when I work my lips up and down his finger a few times before releasing it with a pop. "You just love fucking me," he responds.

"Hmm," I moan as I grind down on his shaft that's still inside of me. "I do love fucking you."

"It's a start..." he says.

"But I would also love you if you lost your cock," I tell him. When Miles opens his mouth to comment, I add, "And your tongue and fingers. You could be a cock-less mute with nubs for hands and I would love you because of the way you look at me and take care of me and protect me. I think I started falling in love with you the day you let me bring home Blackjack. You made me feel really good the night before, but giving me the puppy was...sweet. The only body part you used was your heart."

"Not sure I have one of those," he mutters.

I place my palm overtop of the left side of his chest where his heart is still racing. "You do. I knew it before I felt it."

Grasping my hips and then moving his hands lower until they're resting on my lower belly, he says, "If I have a heart, then it'll be relocated for the next few months."

"See!" I say as I lean down to kiss his lips with tears blurring my vision. "This is what I'm talking about."

"I'm gonna miss you both," Miles says when I pull back.

"We're gonna miss you too," I tell him as one of the tears overflows and slides down my cheek. "Be careful."

"Don't worry about me. I'll be fucking fine."

"I hope so," I tell him before we kiss, tongues tangling until his phone starts to ring from the cut we tossed aside.

"I better get that," he says with a heavy sigh, so I ease off of him and lay on my side while he pulls out his phone from his cut and puts it to his ear. "Yeah?" he answers while watching me. "Okay, we're at Eddie's. See you then."

After he ends the call, Miles tells me, "Sasha and Mercy are on their way."

"How long? Enough for one more time?" I ask.

"Fuck yes," Miles growls as he climbs on top of me and runs the tip of his tongue over my nipple while watching my face. "They'll just have to wait for us to finish, because this next round is going to last a long damn time."

～

"I'LL BE CALLING and checking in with you whenever I can," Miles promises me with another quick kiss on my lips before he opens the rear passenger door of the SUV. After putting my suitcase inside, he stands back for me to climb in.

"Take care of yourself. Love you," he says when I'm seated inside.

"Love you. Be careful!" I say again before he shuts the door. "Sorry to keep you waiting. I'm Kira," I tell the two women in the front seat. The driver is a beautiful redhead who could easily be a movie star, and the passenger is a gorgeous blonde woman.

"Hi, Kira. I'm Sasha, and this is Mercy," the passenger says while gesturing to the driver, who pulls away and out of the salvage yard. "We've both been there at the newlywed stage. Ah, I miss those days," she says with a sigh.

"So, um, are you two the only other women?" I ask.

"Oh, no. Lexi, Nova, Audrey and their kids are all riding together in Torin's van. Never thought I would say Torin and van in the same sentence." Sasha pauses for a moment to giggle before continuing on. "Anyway, we're going to pick up Peyton, and then we'll head for South Carolina."

"Oh, okay," I reply. "I guess this trip will give me a chance to meet everyone."

"You'll love these ladies," Mercy says. "And now that you're part of the Kings' family, they would bend over backward to help you."

"We should go see Cynthia as soon as we get back into town," Sasha says. "Want to come with me?"

"Absolutely," Mercy agrees. "They think she's going to be okay?"

"She made it out of surgery, so the doctors believe the worst is over. Now it's time for *a lot* of healing."

"Ah, who is Cynthia? What happened to her?" I ask them.

"Miles didn't tell you?" Sasha looks over her seat to ask me.

"No."

"She's Reece's girlfriend. Earlier today she was kidnapped by her abusive ex and he tried to kill her."

"Oh, my god," I gasp. "And she's going to be okay?"

"They had to take her into surgery and she's going to be in pain for a while, but yeah, it looks like she's out of the woods."

"That's good," I say. "Did they catch the ex yet?"

"Yeah. He's dead," Mercy answers. "Cops took him down."

"Good," I mutter.

The girls laugh and then Sasha says, "I think you're going to fit in with this group just fine."

"Do either of you know what the latest crisis is? Abe won't tell me anything except 'everything is fine' which I know is bullshit. His eyes looked like they were gonna pop out of his head when he was throwing all my things in a bag," Mercy says.

"No clue," Sasha says. "Chase was a nervous-sweaty mess but wouldn't tell me anything either. It must be big though if they're sending all of us out of town. I had to give up my exclusive political corruption story too!"

"I, ah, I know what happened," I tell them.

"Spill, girl," Sasha says when she looks back at me.

"It's my fault, so I'm sorry you're having to leave home and that your men are involved."

"Your fault?" Mercy asks.

"My father gave up Miles' name to the Russian mafia. Then, when some of their men showed up at our house, Miles killed all four of them."

"Oh fuck," Sasha whispers. "The Russian mafia? That's not big. It sounds like a gigantic shitstorm. They're coming for the Kings now?" she asks, voice hoarse with emotion.

"Yes, but Miles said something about ambushing the Russian

boss. They'll go after them first before they can attack the Kings. They'll be dead before they know what hit them."

"God, I hope it works," Mercy says.

"Me too," Sasha agrees. "I've seen one Kings' war and could gladly go the rest of my life without enduring another."

CHAPTER THIRTY-ONE

Miles

"So ʜᴏᴡ ɪs this all going down?" Chase asks Torin after all the bikes in our convoy are parked outside an old, worn-down warehouse in Greensboro and all of us have followed him inside.

"That's what we're about to talk to Ivan about," our president replies. "He's running this show and he got Kozlov here. Now, we need to find out how he thinks we should proceed to take these guys out."

The warehouse looks like some type of old training gym for fighters with punching bags hanging all around and a ragged looking boxing ring in the center.

"Welcome to my town, gentlemen," a young black-haired guy in a pinstripe suit says when he strolls into the main room, surrounded by an entourage of five huge, bodybuilder size men who I'm guessing are his guards.

"Ivan, it's nice to finally meet you face to face," Torin says when he walks over and offers him a handshake.

"You too," Ivan responds. "This everyone?"

"No," Torin says. "This is only a third of my men. We've got our Charlotte charter coming up in an hour, and the Raleigh charter an hour after they get here, trying to space out all the bikes. Forty-five bikers showing up at one time may look suspicious."

"Good idea," Ivan agrees.

"So when and where is this meet up gonna happen?" Torin asks with his hands on his hips, ready to get down to business.

"I think I've worked out the best possible place to avoid innocent casualties," Ivan starts. "Escapades is our local strip club. A man like Kozlov can't resist free tits and ass, so we're gonna feed him and his twelve men, liquor them up, and then my girls will offer him and his men some...companionship. The dancers will take them one at a time into our six private rooms. That's where your crew can be waiting."

"That sounds like a good plan so far," Torin replies. "Will the girls be in on this?"

"They will," Ivan tells him with a nod. "And we'll make sure they escort the men in first, then shut the door behind them, leaving them in the dark. I'm guessing your men have silencers?"

"We do," Torin says.

"Good. Two of your guys waiting in each room will be plenty. Once the girls play their part, they'll head out the back exit. I trust these girls, but even if I didn't, they won't see or hear anything. They may make their own assumptions, but there's nothing to worry about there."

"Okay," Torin agrees.

"For any of the remaining Russians sitting in the main room, I have a plan for them too," Ivan explains. "After your men take care of business in the private rooms, they can head backstage without being seen. I'll have the DJ announce for the girls to go backstage for their group dance number, cue the song we agree will be our signal, and then your guys come out on stage and cut the rest down."

"That should work for the fewest casualties on our side," Torin agrees, making my stomach roll at the thought of us losing a King for the shit I dragged them into.

"Did I mention I don't allow weapons in my establishment?" Ivan asks with a grin.

"Jesus Christ," Torin says with a swipe of his palm down his face. "They'll be sitting ducks."

"They will," Ivan agrees. "But no one will miss these drug-pushing thugs who flood my city and others up and down the coast with heroin."

"True," Torin agrees. "What about local law enforcement and clean up?"

"I'll have my men dispose of the Russians and clean up the club so fast we'll be open to the public for business again by tomorrow night," he says. "And the local police officers love Escapades so much, they would sell their souls to keep it open. Several would call to check in with me before showing up even if someone calls it in."

"Wow, then I guess you've thought of everything," Torin tells him.

"Just one question left," Ivan says. "Who wants Kozlov?"

"Me," I speak up and say as I take a step forward to stand next to Torin. "He came after my in-laws and then sent his men after me and my wife. I want to be the one who watches the life drain from his eyes so I can tell my wife he won't be bothering us or her parents again."

Giving me a nod of understanding, Ivan says, "In that case, you'll want to hunker down in the champagne room. Nothing but the best for our Russian mob boss."

"Perfect," I agree.

CHAPTER THIRTY-TWO

Kira

"Make yourself at home, Mrs. Fury," Rory, the president of the Myrtle Beach Savage Kings' charter, says after he let us into the beachfront mansion and shows us around. "Both of the kitchens are fully stocked; but if there's anything else you or the other ladies need, here's my number." He hands a white business card to the small, dark-haired woman who I now know is Lexi. I take it she must be in charge. "Make a list if you need to and we'll send our prospects shopping."

"Thank you so much for your hospitality. This place is amazing," Lexi tells him with her baby girl propped on her hip, sucking on a pacifier and twirling her mother's hair around her finger. The pang of longing to hold my own baby in my arms seems to grow stronger every second.

"Anything for the Furys and our mother charter," Rory says. "There will be no less than four of my crew on the grounds at all time. Even if you don't see them, they'll be here, patrolling. They won't bother you unless it's important and even then, they'll ring the doorbell. Torin said a few of the old ladies are packing heat."

"That's right. We can take care of ourselves," Sasha says before she grabs the baby out of Lexi's arms. "Now, all we need is to find some shows to binge while we try to distract ourselves for the next few days."

"Good luck with that," Rory replies. "I'll show myself out."

"Thank you!" we all call out to him as he gets on the elevator, that's right, an elevator in the private home, and takes it down to the ground floor.

The ladies all sigh heavily once he's out of sight as their shoulders deflate, knowing it's going to be a tough few days while we wait for our men to return.

"How do you all do it?" I ask them. "Not go crazy when they're gone?"

"Thankfully, it doesn't happen often," Lexi says. "Which one is yours again? Sax or Cooper?"

"Ah, Miles," I respond.

"Miles?" she repeats with her brow raised in surprise. "Seriously?"

"We're married and expecting," I say with my hand going down to my lower belly.

"Aww! Congratulations!" Sasha says, giving me a hug before the other women follow suit.

"Welcome to the family," a young girl around my age says. "I'm Audrey, War's sister and Maddox's wife."

"Nice to meet you," I tell her.

"And I'm Torin's wife by the way," Lexi says after our embrace.

"Torin is the president of the Kings," Sasha informs me.

"Oh, okay," I say. "Miles hasn't really told me much about the MC. All I know is he spends a lot of time at the Savage Asylum. What exactly is that?"

"That's the clubhouse," Mercy informs me. "Let's all have a seat, girl, so we can fill you in."

"Thanks, I would appreciate that since Miles hasn't," I tell them. "I think he was worried I couldn't handle it, but I can."

"Of course you can," Sasha says. "Our men think we're fragile females who freak out over the smallest thing. The truth is, it takes a strong woman to bring a King to his knees, but once he's there, he'll treat you like a queen and do anything for you."

"I'm starting to see that," I admit as we all take a seat on the sectional.

"So, start from the beginning," Lexi says. "How did you and Miles end up together?"

"Well, he saved my father's life," I tell them honestly, deciding to leave out the part about the arranged marriage since I get the feeling that Miles doesn't want anyone to know.

"That's so sweet," Audrey says with her fist propped up on her chin. "I didn't know he had a soft side."

"Oh, you should've seen him stuff a puppy into his cut. It was the funniest and most adorable thing ever!"

For the rest of the night, the women and I bond over shared stories about our tough guys, and have fun playing with Lexi's kids and War's son Ren.

And for the first time ever, I feel like I've finally figured out what I want to do with the rest of my life – *this*. I was meant to be the wife of a Savage King, the mother of his child, and friends with all of the other 'old ladies.'

Now I just hope my husband and their men all come back to us after they finish handling their business with the Russians.

Miles

ONCE ALL OF the Kings from the other charters arrived, Ivan's guards drove us all over to *Escapades* in three ridiculous stretch limousines. "I haven't been in one of these since I was stationed out at Camp Lejeune," I remark during the ride.

"I don't remember any limos on base," Torin grunts.

"Not at the base, at the strip club in Jacksonville," I grin at him. "You know what they use these for, don't you?"

"I can guess," Torin snorts. He's being snippy, but I know it's only because he's worried about his Kings and what's about to go down.

"The limousines are for mobile prostitution," Ivan interjects. "Supposedly, of course. On the books, the club offers them as a private lounge for one-on-one time with the girls, in a more relaxed atmosphere than the club can provide. Practically, they give us plausible deniability, as we can't be seen to have women selling sexual favors in the club itself."

"You condone that sort of thing?" Torin glowers.

"Not personally, no," Ivan replies, seeming completely unoffended at Torin's gruff tone. "It's just a reality of the sex industry. The women who are willing to do such things will do it regardless of my feelings on the matter, so the best thing I can do for them is make sure they have the resources they need to do it in a responsible manner. It makes the girls and the patrons happy, and I can't deny that it's fairly lucrative."

"Even after the cleaning bills?" Chase grins.

"Oh, we don't bother with that," Ivan replies, immediately wiping the smile off of Chase's face.

"He's kidding, right?" Chase says weakly as he stands up as much as the low ceiling will allow, rubbing a hand across the leather seat. "Oh god, it feels moist," he groans, quickly swiping his hand across his jeans.

"That's just your sweaty ass," Torin barks. "Of course he's kidding. Sit down, shut up, and get your head in the game. If you get hurt, Sasha will murder me."

"And don't ever say 'moist' again," Dalton laughs. "You're going to ruin strippers for all of us with that kind of talk. God, I hate that word."

Despite Torin's warning, our banter continues until the limos pull into the back parking lot of a huge stucco building covered in multi-colored neon tubing. We quickly make our way inside, the interior of the building looking sterile and uninviting without the black lights or any of the normal club ambience currently on display.

"Where's the champagne room?" I ask Ivan immediately, eager to get settled.

"I'll show you all to the private rooms," Ivan replies. "You're not planning to deal with Kozlov alone, are you? No reason to take any unnecessary chances."

"He won't be alone," Torin interrupts. "Sax, you're with Miles. Keep him from ruining the room, will you? We want Kozlov dead, but we don't need his guts hanging from the ceiling."

Sax nods in agreement, then we follow Ivan down the hall with the rest of the Kings. Sax is a good pick for a partner. We're brothers in the club, but not close friends. He spends more time out on his boat than on his motorcycle, making runs up and down the coast. He's our smuggler, and I know he's got the guts to handle any dirty jobs that come his way.

The champagne room is just as gaudy as you would expect. The walls are covered in wood panels painted with golden designs. Spotlights set in the ceiling highlight a glass shower stall set in one corner, while a hot tub burbles merrily across from it.

Peeking his head inside, Dalton says, "Oh dude, you should totally hide in the hot tub. You could explode up from the water, then grab him and stuff his face into a jet!"

"I would prefer we leave the hot tub out of this," Ivan sighs.

"They're not going to be here for another hour, anyhow, dipshit," I tell Dalton. "You think Sax and I want to soak our nuts together while we wait?"

"Hell no," Sax says before Dalton can reply.

With a small nod, Ivan backs out of the room and starts to pull the door closed. "Remember, when they arrive outside, we'll start the music. Once you hear us switch to an AC/DC album, they'll be on their way to the room."

"AC/DC, got it," Sax nods as he takes a seat on the single, high-backed wooden chair in the room. It looks more like a prop for the dancers rather than a functional piece of furniture, but it holds the smaller man's weight without creaking. That leaves the weary-looking loveseat for me.

Once I sink down into the cushion and realize how uncomfortable it is, I see that Sax made the right decision. I lean forward and ask him, "You okay with all this? You spend most of your time offshore, and I feel kind of bad dragging you in for this shitshow."

"Yeah, of course, Miles," Sax replies, his eyebrows rising in surprise. "Are *you* okay? It's not like you to be, I don't know... concerned for my feelings."

"I'm good, man. Hell, I'm probably the best I've ever been in my life. This girl, Kira, she's something else. Hooking up with her sort of led to all this shit, though, and I just don't want any of you guys holding it against her."

"Shit, man, I know, don't worry. You're the knucklehead that offed those Russians and led us down this road." Sax laughs, waving a hand to stop me before I can protest. "I don't blame anyone. We all chose this life willingly, knowing full well there would be days like this. I can't promise I'm going to like your girl, though."

"What do you mean by that?" I demand, instantly offended on her behalf.

"Whatever she did to you made you chattier than my granny at church. If I had known you were going to be this 'talkie', I would have asked to be paired with Dalton."

"Now that's god-damned offensive," I reply with a chuckle. "You take that back and I'll settle down, all right? I just wanted everyone to know that I'm responsible for this, and I appreciate the help cleaning the shit up."

"Yeah, yeah, save it for the table," Sax says as he crosses his arms and leans the chair back against the wall. "Look, the plan is solid. All we have to do is be cool for a bit, handle our business, and I can get home in time to get dinner with One-Eye and catch the tide."

"Who the hell is 'One-Eye'? I know you ain't running around with a chick with that nick-name."

"Nah, man, One-Eye is my cat," he says. "Found it on a wharf down in Tijuana. He had been scrapping with something and had lost an eye and an ear to it. I fed him part of a tamale I had bought out on the street, and after that he wouldn't stop following me around. He came on board the boat, and he's lived with me ever since."

I stare at Sax in silence after he finished talking, until he finally shifts his chair forward in irritation and demands, "What?"

"Of all the things you could have picked up in Tijuana, you got a Mexican cat!" I laugh. "Does he understand any English, or did you have to learn some Spanish to call him?"

"He's a damned cat, you dumbass, not a Mexican," Sax scowled. "You sure this Kira chick didn't give you some sort of disease that makes you fucking weird?"

"Maybe she did," I sigh as I sink back into the couch. "If you count love as a disease, then yeah, I think I might have it."

"All right, that's it," Sax groans. "One more line like that and I'm not going to sit with Dalton, I'm going to send him in here to sit with *you*."

I can't believe I'm still laughing, or how giddy I feel even in our current circumstances. I honor Sax's request, though, and we sit together listening as the club DJ gets the sound system set up and begins shuffling through his playlist. I'm surprised at how well Sax handles the waiting as the minutes drag out into the first hour. I served as a sniper, so I can sit still all day waiting on the perfect opportunity. I didn't expect Sax to have that kind of discipline, but I'm pleasantly surprised when he remains focused and uncomplaining as we listen eagerly for every change of song.

After what feels like an eternity, AC/DC's "Back in Black" begins booming from the speakers. Sax is on his feet immediately, his pistol with the suppressor in place already in his hand. "I'll kill the lights and stand by the switch," he says. "When she closes him in here, I'll flip them on, and back up your play."

I nod to him and take my place on the far side of the door, both of us out of sight from the hallway. When the door swings open and light from the hall spills in, we hear a feminine giggle followed by, "Go on in, baby. I'll grab the lights and get this party started!"

I hear a heavy grunt that might be something in Russian just before the door slams shut, leaving us all in the pitch darkness for a split second before Sax flips on the lights. Standing before me is a tall, lean man with a badly receding hairline, still smiling in anticipation of his upcoming 'champagne special.'

As his eyes meet mine, he looks puzzled, but before he can fully register who I am or what I'm doing inside the dark room, I raise my pistol and fire twice, directly into his forehead. No words were spoken or needed, and the assassination is over within three seconds of Kozlov entering the room.

His body collapses to the shaggy carpet in a limp heap, the expression on his face frozen in vague surprise and confusion. "Quick and efficient," Sax nods. "Good to see your girl hasn't changed that about you. Wasn't there anything you wanted to ask him, though?"

"No. There was nothing that motherfucker could say that would change what he did to my wife and her family. You don't reason with people like this," I add, going over to kick Kozlov's leg. "You just put them down and go on about your business. Speaking of which, it sounds like we're being called to the stage for our dance."

Sax nods to the speaker, where the DJ is calling out a list of obvious stage names, asking "Jasmine, Onyx, and Steel to make their way to the main stage." We duck into the hallway, which is now filled with other Savage Kings, all of their faces resolute and stony, thankfully still in one piece. Without speaking, we file down the back hallway to the curtained stage, fanning out as we wait for our cue.

Once we're in position, with the sounds of the Russian's raucous laughter only a few feet away from us, Ivan nods to someone at the side of the stage. Instead of opening slowly, the curtain drops from the ceiling, suddenly revealing our huge group of leather clad warriors crowded onto the stage. The group of gang members gathered only a few feet away barely have time to gasp before a hail of bullets descends upon them, a dozen corpses flying out of their chairs to the floor below us.

"Make sure they're dead," Torin orders as the Savage Kings leap off the stage, moving amongst the bodies. "We good?" he asks a moment later as our men check on the Russians, twice administering a coup de grace to at least two of the men on the ground.

"We're clear," Chase finally replies. "Ivan, you still want us to pile the bodies up in the kitchen?"

"That would be ideal," Ivan says, stepping down from the stage. "If you'll have your men check, they'll find some large rolls of plastic wrap for the bodies in my office. Wrap the bodies and take them through the kitchen to the loading dock. I arranged to have a delivery made to our kitchen this afternoon. We'll back the truck up, unload our necessities, and then send our recently departed guests off to their final rest."

"You sure you don't need our help getting rid of the bodies?" Torin asks.

"Don't worry about that. We have an arrangement with a local crematorium just for this sort of special occasion. By this time tomorrow, all of this will just be a dusty memory, scattered to the wind."

"Let's get this done, then," Sax says from just behind me, slapping me on the shoulder. "The sooner we wrap these boys up, the sooner you can get back to your honeymoon."

"Hell yes," I sigh in relief, "and you can get back to your little One-Eyed pussy, right?"

"Your *what?*" Dalton's laughter is jarring as we stand amongst the pile of bodies. "Oh shit, Miles, tell us, tell us! You can't just say something like that and walk off."

"You better," Sax warns me. "Not a word to that one; I'll never hear the end of it."

"Shut up and start wrapping!" Torin snaps. "I've got a wife and kids waiting on me, and I don't intend to spend a second longer than I have to smelling these stinking Russian guts!"

"Yes, daddy," Dalton says with a roll of his eyes as he bends down to grab a body.

I help him as we begin to finish up our grim work. Inwardly, I feel like I'm flying, more elated and freer than I can remember ever feeling before in my life.

CHAPTER THIRTY-THREE

Kira

"Shh," Sasha says when she stands up abruptly in the middle of the living room. "Turn the television down."

Lexi grabs the remote and mutes the afternoon news. Sasha had wanted to check and see who picked up the story she had hoped to scoop.

"Do you hear that?" Sasha asks once the house is quiet.

"Thunder?" Nova asks with her brow furrowed.

"No," Sasha responds with a grin spreading across her face. "That's not thunder. That's a convoy of Harleys!"

"Let's go see!" Audrey squeals from the kitchen table where she's been playing checkers with War's son Ren. Jumping up from her chair, she grabs his small hand, pulling him along as they race down the stairs with the rest of us following behind. I'm bringing up the rear since running down stairs and pregnancy don't mix very well. It may be early, but I've already developed the 'clumsies' my mother warned me she had while pregnant after I told her our good news on the phone last night. And I've already grown pretty damn attached to our little bean.

"It could just be more of the Myrtle Beach guys, right?" Peyton, Dalton's wife, says from beside me on the steps like she's trying not to get her hopes up. "Do you really think they're back already?"

"God, I hope so," I tell her.

When we walk out the front door and gather around with the rest of the women, our four Myrtle Beach Kings are opening the gated entrance to let a herd of black motorcycles into the driveway.

My chest grows heavy with my racing pulse as I hold my breath waiting for Miles to come riding up. One by one the women disperse, going to their men.

And I could slap Miles for being one of the last riders to pull in.

"Thank god," I say in relief. I'm down the steps and beside his bike before his helmet is off. "You're okay. Is everyone...are the rest of the guys okay?" I ask in concern. I've become friends with these women and really don't want to be the cause of anyone's heartache.

"Hell yeah," Miles says, reaching his arm out to pull me to him before he even stands up from the seat. Our lips collide, and then we're grabbing and pulling frantically at each other as our tongues delve in and out of each other's mouths.

When Miles grips my shoulders to push me away from him, it's only long enough for him to throw his leg over his bike; and then he's hefting me up in his arms and my legs are around his waist.

"Tell me which bedroom is yours so I can rip your clothes off," he growls as he carries me toward the front door.

"But –" I start to ask if it's the time or place with so many other people around us. Then I glance over the driveway and see it's empty. I guess we're not the only ones with the same plan. Hopefully someone thought to take the kids to the beach. "Second floor, last door on the left," I respond.

We kiss the whole way up the stairs, and then finally we're in a room. I'm not entirely certain if it's my room or someone else's, and right now I don't care, because Miles lowers me to the bed and then his hard body is on top of mine.

"I missed you," I tell him while attempting to remove his cut at the same time he's pulling my shirt off over my head.

"You have no fucking idea how much I missed you," Miles tells me, dark eyes staring into mine. Eyes that I once thought were scary and intimidating are now comforting from my fierce protector.

"I love you," he mumbles gruffly before his gaze lowers, his lips and tongue teasing my breast while he unhooks my bra and tosses it away. I've already learned that my protector doesn't like to be vulnerable, so my heart swells whenever he is.

"I love you too," I tell him as his mouth moves lower to gently kiss my belly while his rough hands tear off my bottoms.

Miles stands up long enough to remove every piece of his own clothing. My mouth waters at the sight of his sculpted chest and abs. And just seeing his thick cock jutting upward, hard and ready for me nearly has me moaning. I'm so hot for him that I can't wait any longer. My fingers reach down between my thighs, needing to touch myself while I wait for Miles to return to me.

"Goddamn, you are so fucking sexy," he groans before his knees hit the mattress and he's crawling up between my legs. His head dips down and the flat of his wet tongue licks all the way up my slit and stops at my fingers. I scissor them apart, holding myself open for him as he kisses and sucks and laps at my clit. The pleasure builds so hard and fast that I'm pretty sure I levitate off the mattress when Miles has me soaring into what can only be described as heaven on earth.

Miles

I LOVE EATING my wife out and could keep my tongue inside of her for hours. But first, I need to be inside of her, claiming my pussy and showing her just how much this cock she owns loves and missed her.

Before her beautiful blue eyes reopen from her orgasm, I'm kneeling between her legs and thrusting inside of her.

"*OH GOD!*" Kira shouts as her back arches underneath me. When her eager little hips start lifting urgently to slam her pussy on my cock, meeting each of my thrusts, she makes me feel like a goddamn deity. "*More! Harder! Yes!*" she exclaims while her fingernails dig into my back, pulling my chest down to hers.

I try to kiss her, but it's impossible thanks to our frantic fucking.

Then, her blue eyes open and lock with mine. Kira stares into my soul so intensely while our bodies are joined, looking for the answer to a question she hasn't asked me yet.

Finally, she speaks.

"Did you...did you...kill anyone?" she asks through gasps.

"Yes," I answer without hesitation when I continue to pound inside of her as deep as I can go. "I put a fucking bullet right between Kozlov's eyes."

Her lips part on a gasp and her pussy squeezes my shaft even tighter.

"God, that's so...so...*hot*," she moans just as her body clamps down on my cock and throbs with the pleasure taking her over the edge.

My lips slant over hers, the woman I love. The woman who loves me, even my darkness. Our tongues tangle as my hips pump three more times before I surrender to the ecstasy.

"Thank you," Kira whispers as we both lie there, still connected as our hearts recover and slow.

"Are you thanking me for the fuck...or for the killing?" I ask when I look down at her with a teasing grin.

"Both. Everything," she replies as her fingernails come up to graze either side of my head.

"No thanks necessary," I tell her. "I would do anything for you and our kid. Now I finally get it, why I was born to be a killer, to hurt my enemies without blinking an eye. My whole life I've just been training for this, to keep the people I love safe."

EPILOGUE

Miles

Six months later...

"You ARE SO FUCKING WHIPPED," Chase says when he and Abe come up to the refreshment station. "If the rest of the guys could see you now, serving punch at a chick's baby shower, they would never let you live it down."

"I'm whipped?" I repeat. With the ladle in my hand, I slowly pour two cups of the lime sherbet punch and then hand each of the assholes one. "This party is for *my* wife and *my* kid. So, what the fuck are you two jackasses doing at a baby shower?"

"Sasha and Mercy made us," Abe grumbles before he throws back his punch. "Damn, that's good. Can I get a refill?" he asks, holding out his cup for me.

"Sure," I reply. "Would you like a pink and blue napkin with baby strollers on it to wipe your lime mustache too?"

Cursing, he quickly swipes his hand over his facial hair.

"You know," I say as I spot their two old ladies in the crowd, both looking like they have basketballs stuffed under their shirts. "You two actually owe me for helping you finally knock up your women. Guess giving your dicks a break while we dealt with the Russians was just what the fertility doctor ordered."

"No shit," Chase agrees with a snort. "And the second trimester is awesome. Sasha wants all the sex she can get and there's no pressure to knock her up."

"Fuck yeah, man," Abe agrees with a fist bump.

"Oh, just wait," I warn them as I locate Kira sitting in the middle of the group of women, slouched in her chair with her hand rubbing her enormous belly. Sweat is dripping down her face; and while I can't see them, I'm betting her shoes are off because her feet are so swollen, she can't stand to have them on for more than a few minutes. She may be miserable as hell right now, but she's still so goddamn gorgeous carrying my child that she takes my breath away.

"I'm guessing the horny days end soon?" Abe asks. "Your girl looks like she wants to punch someone in the nuts, probably you."

"The horny days end, but now we're in the fucking three or four times a day phase to try and get the kid out."

"That really work?" Chase asks.

"No clue, but that doesn't mean I'll stop trying," I reply with a grin. "Did I mention I knocked up Kira on the first try?"

"That doesn't count," Abe mutters. "You weren't trying to put a baby in her. It *always* happens when you don't plan on it and don't wear a rubber. Every fool knows that."

"You're just jealous," I tell him. "My boys are stronger swimmers than yours."

"Your boys probably carry AK-47s and wear bandanas," Chase says with a chuckle. "I bet they blew right through that pussy like it was a hostile takeover."

"Fuck yeah," I agree.

"Miles!" Kira yells for me while holding a present over her head. "Come here! You know I can't get up without a tow truck!"

"Coming, princess," I say as I put the ladle down and make my way through the crowd of women. "What do you need?" I ask when I crouch down in front of her.

"This one's for you," she says, smiling at me when she hands me the gift.

"Me?" I ask. "I thought this was supposed to be a party for baby stuff."

"It is," she responds. "But this one is from me to you." With a wince, she adds, "I peeked at the gender last week."

Gasping indignantly, I ask, "What happened to we're gonna wait and be surprised?" I've wanted to know the sex from the first ultrasound appointment, but Kira convinced me to wait.

"I know. I'm sorry," she apologizes. "So, open it and then you'll know what we're having too."

"Here, you can have my seat," her mom says when she stands up.

After the shit with Kozlov went down, and finding out their daughter was pregnant, Kira's parents decided to rebuild their furniture business in Wilmington instead of Charleston. They're good in-laws and Kira loves having them close. They even seem to approve of me. Guess it helped that I severed their ties with the Russians once and for all.

Taking Kira's mom's chair, I rip into the pink and blue wrapping paper and then lift the lid off the cardboard box.

Inside is a bunch of tissue paper I have to remove before I get to the answer of the question that's been driving me crazy – are we having a girl or a boy?

Finally, I see it. Such a tiny little thing – a bright pink leather cut with the Savage Kings logo and words on the back. It's so small it fits in the flat of my palm.

"A girl? We're having a girl?" I glance over and ask Kira.

"We're having a girl," she says with her blue eyes shining with unshed happy tears as I wrap my arm around her shoulders to pull her to me.

Even though she never said which gender she really wanted, I'm not blind. Kira spends a lot more time looking at the baby girl clothes in stores. And I'm so happy she's getting what she wanted. It's perfect actually, because she's already given me everything I've ever needed.

The End

I never thought I would be stupid enough to make a deal with the devil, but here I am doing just that.

It's not like he really gave me a choice. I have to give the Governor what he wants, or he's going to throw all of my Savage Kings MC brothers into prison for decades.

And what exactly does Governor Satan need from me? That's the real kicker because he's insisting that I...date his daughter. No, not just date her. He wants me to convince Isobel to stop spiraling out of control before she ends up dead, or worse – ruin her father's chance at getting re-elected.

I have no clue why his beautiful wild child is partying her way through life, crossing off items on a mile-long bucket list, and I don't really care.

Somehow, someway, I have to convince her to put down roots and go back to being the picture-perfect good girl her father raised.

As if I'm not in deep enough, I've never wanted anyone more than the free-spirit who refuses to spend her short life standing in one place for too long. Too bad Isobel is going to hate my guts when she finds out I'm the asshole who has to lock her back up in a cage.

And if I fail to do so, well, there won't be an orange jumpsuit waiting for me. I'll never make it to prison because the Governor dug up all my dirt that I thought I had carefully buried. If he tells the Kings that I started prospecting with them as a DEA rat ten years ago, they'll never forgive me. How could they when I still haven't forgiven myself?

Order your copy of Sax now!

ABOUT THE AUTHORS

New York Times and *USA Today* bestselling author Lane Hart and husband D.B. West were both born and raised in North Carolina. They still live in the south with their two daughters and enjoy spending the summers on the beach and watching football in the fall.

Connect with D.B.:
Twitter: https://twitter.com/AuthorDBWest
Facebook: https://www.facebook.com/authordbwest/
Website: http://www.dbwestbooks.com
Email: dbwestauthor@outlook.com

Connect with Lane:
Twitter: https://twitter.com/WritingfromHart
Facebook: http://www.facebook.com/lanehartbooks
Instagram: https://www.instagram.com/authorlanehart/
Website: http://www.lanehartbooks.com
Email: lane.hart@hotmail.com

Join Lane's Facebook group to read books before they're released, help choose covers, character names, and titles of books! https://www.facebook.com/groups/bookboyfriendswanted/

Sign up for Lane and D.B.'s newsletter to get updates on new releases and freebies!

Made in the USA
Monee, IL
27 December 2022

23268906R00125